ENCHANTED
MISADVENTURES
WITH
GREAT-AUNT POPPY

MAGIC, MAYHEM, AND MONSTERS

WHAT OTHERS ARE SAYING ABOUT

ENCHANTED MISADVENTURES WITH GREAT-AUNT POPPY

Spooky, fun, and perfect for kids looking for an adventure! It made me laugh, gasp, and wonder what would happen next. This book has everything you'd want for the younger generation. I'm excited to see what the author writes next.

—Victoria McCombs, best-selling author of *The Storyteller's Daughter*

ENCHANTED MISADVENTURES WITH GREAT-AUNT POPPY

MAGIC, MAYHEM, AND MONSTERS

HALLIE CHRISTENSEN

SWEETWATER
BOOKS

An imprint of Cedar Fort, Inc.
Springville, Utah

ISBN 13: 978-1-4621-4048-0

Published by Sweetwater Books, an imprint of Cedar Fort, Inc.
2373 W. 700 S., Springville, UT, 84663
Distributed by Cedar Fort, Inc., www.cedarfort.com

Library of Congress Control Number: 2021939437

Cover design by Courtney Proby
Cover design © 2021 Cedar Fort, Inc.
Edited by Hali Bird

Printed in the United States of America

10 9 8 7 6 5 4 3 2 1

Printed on acid-free paper

For my family, both with and without paws.

1

THE ALEXANDER CHILDREN USUALLY ENJOYED HOLIDAY BREAKS, BUT this one was different.

Their parents would not be with them. They would not be in their cozy home all decorated for Christmas with their bright green tree and red stockings. And, they wouldn't be able to do all their festive family traditions—making a gingerbread house, driving around at night to look at lights and drinking hot chocolate, or watching favorite holiday movies. This Christmas was different. This Christmas, they were forced to spend a week with Great-Aunt Poppy.

"Was she the only person that said she could watch us?" Ava, the eldest child, pleaded helplessly in the middle seat of the car. She was the sole kid out of the family who had actually seen Great-Aunt Poppy and been to her house. The best way to describe the house was haunted. The best way to describe Poppy was absolutely horrifying, down to her pointed hat and mole-covered face. Her real name may have been Great-Aunt Poppy, but after that one terrifying experience, Ava secretly gave her the nickname Groppy because, as she thought, *she looks like a Groppy.* And after hearing her frightening tale, her siblings agreed.

"This was such short notice, Ava. We're just fortunate and grateful that we found someone to watch all three of you." Her mom turned around from the passenger seat and gave a consoling look. "I'm sure you will have a great time."

Ava was positive she would not.

Six-year-old Charlotte put on a good show crying buckets of tears, but her mom knew crocodile tears when she saw them.

"Those are fake tears, Charlotte." Her mom sighed. "You're not fooling me."

Charlotte glowered. It wasn't only that she was terrified by the thought of staying with her creepy great-aunt, but she had just gotten new caticorn sheets on her bed and was pretty sure the house they were going to would not have those same bedsheets. She loved cats and unicorns, so the caticorn was obviously the perfect animal. How was she supposed to sleep without hundreds of caticorns around her?

"Are you sure you have to go to work?" Charlotte asked her parents sweetly while trying to make her brown eyes as large and kitten-like as possible. Since the tears hadn't worked, Charlotte would try her second weapon—her eyes. Being the youngest and cutest, she was usually able to get her parents to change their minds about certain things. Especially when it came to things like staying up late, getting another sparkly cat shirt, or receiving a second helping of chocolate cake. But being cute wasn't working today.

"Charlotte, sweetie, I am sorry, but Daddy and I have to go to work. We'll only be gone a week. There are a lot of people that need us to help them. I'm sure they would like to be with their families, too, instead of being sick at the hospital."

Charlotte crossed her arms fiercely, making her brown ringlets bounce by the sides of her head where they were tied in two pigtails. She pouted in her car seat as she jerked her head to look outside at Christmas decorations. There was nothing Charlotte could do to change their minds.

Ava sighed and leaned her head against the cold glass of the car window, letting her breath fog it over so she could draw sad faces with tears. Her dark blonde hair fell into her face and she pushed it away, revealing sorrowful green eyes. Ava turned to her sister sympathetically.

"If the pros and cons list I made won't change their minds, then nothing will. Not even your puppy-dog eyes."

"They're *kitten* eyes," Charlotte corrected her and sniffed.

Ava understood her parents had to go to work. They were doctors and too many people had gotten the flu. This holiday season was not a season of joy but of germs and bacteria. That's why she had been extra careful at school. Ava hated germs. *Hated* them. She carried hand sanitizer on her backpack, and an extra one inside her backpack, and hand wipes in her pocket, just to be safe. At the early age of five, Ava had unequivocally determined that kids were covered in germs and spread them quickly. She dreaded the school bathrooms, pencil sharpeners, doorknobs, lunch trays, and anytime someone handed her a piece of paper after wiping their runny nose with their sleeve. She shivered just thinking about it.

In the middle seat, looking particularly bored with his slicked-back brown hair that Mom had tried to tame that morning, sat the middle child and their only brother, Nolan. He also did not want to go to Groppy's. Nolan would have put up a fight, but it seemed like too much effort when he already knew he wouldn't win. He had at least tried to get sick at school by sitting close to any classmates that sneezed or coughed, but Nolan never seemed to get what he wanted. He was healthy and well and could go to Groppy's.

Nolan's main reason for not wanting to go was his eating habits. Nolan was a picky eater. He liked gross things like zombies, but he certainly did not like eating gross things. And he was pretty sure that gross things were all he would be eating at Groppy's. A whole week of strange, disgusting food. Probably lizard tails and eyeballs or beetle soup. Yuck. He smashed his palms onto his face and groaned.

"I'm going to starve." He held his hands out toward his parents, imploring. "Don't you care about me dying?"

"Nolan, she will have food for you to eat. The only way you would starve is if you refused to eat it," Dad replied without even batting an eye. Nolan groaned again and pretended to die right there in the car, very dramatically. Charlotte poked him in the arm to make sure he wasn't really dead.

"Ow," grunted Nolan. "Just bury me outside by the shed and on my tombstone write the words: *Here lies our favorite child. We should have fed him pizza and let him stay at home.*"

Dad sighed heavily. He wasn't buying it, either.

"You're all acting as if it's the end of the world," Mom said, laughing. "What's so wrong with staying at Aunt Poppy's?"

Everything. Because the Alexander children were positive that Aunt Poppy was a witch.

2

AVA WAS SIX YEARS OLD THE FIRST TIME SHE MET GROPPY. GROPPY was Ava's mother's aunt, making her Ava's great-aunt, meaning she was *really* old. And Ava certainly did not think Groppy was great.

She and her mom had driven to Groppy's house, which was out in the country, surrounded by flat pasture land and thick woods. She lived in a two-story wooden house that, to Ava, looked like it belonged in a scary movie. Paint was chipping off the sides, shutters hung loosely by one good nail, and the steps were crooked and creaked when you stepped on them. The color of the house looked like the same color Ava saw when she cleaned off her paintbrush in a cup of water in art class—a grubby mud puddle. A long, crooked brick chimney puffed out sooty smoke constantly. The house wasn't even straight. It leaned a bit to one side. How it hadn't fallen over, Ava didn't know.

The inside of the house hadn't looked much better. There was a lot of clutter, stacks of papers, scrolls, and books, old pens that looked like feathers, dust-covered blankets piled on top of old, ugly, floral furniture, and tall oak bookcases filled with thousands of books. Perched on all of these were lots and lots of cats that climbed all over the house.

Large, dirty windows let light in the musty old house. When the sun shone through the smudged windows, Ava could see how much dust and cat hair were floating all around her. She had quickly pulled her shirt over her mouth and breathed deeply.

The walls were covered in a striped wallpaper with the most unpleasant color combination Ava had ever seen—brown and burnt orange. And the gross wallpaper was filled with weird portraits. What made it so creepy was that every portrait on the wall had owls in them. Some owls can be fluffy and cute, but these were the kind with sharp slit eyes and pointed beaks, razor-sharp talons, and a wicked glare. They were dark brown or a snow-white, and their eyes seemed to follow Ava wherever she went. She stayed close to her mom during that visit and did not dare leave her side.

And then there was Groppy. She was a shorter plump woman, with thick black hair twisted in a fat, wide braid that hung down her back. She had big moles on her face. Ava found it difficult not to stare at them, but her eyes always moved to those big brown lumps on her aunt's chin, cheeks, and forehead. Especially when there was a hair in one. Groppy's teeth were only a little yellow and crooked, but her breath? *Whew!* It was bad. And let's not forget Groppy's clothes. How no one saw that she was a witch was beyond Ava. Groppy was dressed head to toe in all black clothing. A high-necked button-up black blouse was tucked into a frumpy long black skirt. Everything was black, except for her socks. They were a wildly striped purple and green color, and they bounced off the black outfit like the reflection of the sun off a car window.

Did Ava not see this exact outfit in the dictionary under "witch"? And of course, on top of her head was a pointed black hat. Ava decided that either her mom was blind or Groppy had put a spell on her.

Groppy also smelled strongly of spices, which would have been okay if she didn't also smell strongly of nasty kitty litter. Because she had a billion cats in the house, she had to have a billion litter boxes. The smell was awful.

All of this Ava told her siblings to fully prepare them for the coming week: a spooky and dirty house, tons of cats, musty air, scary portraits, hairy moles, and Groppy. Nolan and Charlotte had gobbled up the horror stories but had hoped that Ava was just overexaggerating.

Since Groppy lived far out in the country, they hadn't had time to go and visit her. It had been years since Ava had been to her creepy, old house, and she silently wished and hoped it wasn't as bad as she remembered.

"Are we close to Groppy's?" Nolan whispered to Ava with a nervous look on his face.

"I think so," Ava replied. "I've seen fewer and fewer houses, and we haven't passed a store in miles, so we're getting close."

"Does she live in the woods?" Charlotte asked, a bit frightened herself. Scary things were known to live in the woods. Ava nodded solemnly, and Charlotte's eyes widened. She was not going to survive this Christmas.

"Now, you kids don't worry about Santa." Mom turned around to smile at them, interrupting their hushed conversation. "We made sure to write a letter and told him you would be staying with Aunt Poppy. Oh, this will be such a fun Christmas. I'm jealous I won't get to celebrate it with you and Aunt Poppy. Out in the beautiful country surrounded by woods. So much fun!"

The children all stared back at their mother with the most disgusted and depressed looks they could manage. Mom took the hint and sighed, turning back around in her seat. Santa finding them on Christmas Eve was the least of their worries. They just wanted to live through the week.

"Can we sleep together?" Charlotte asked her siblings.

"You kick in your sleep," Nolan protested. "If we have to share a bed, I won't be sleeping beside you."

Charlotte whimpered. Ava reached over her rude brother and touched her sister's hand. Charlotte turned to look at her. "I'll sleep by you," Ava said with a smile. That made Charlotte feel much better. Then, Ava winked. "We'll make Nolan sleep with the cats."

Nolan crossed his arms. "Yea, that's not happening."

"We're here!" Dad sang out brightly. The sound of loose gravel crunched beneath the car tires, and the van came to an abrupt halt. All three of the Alexander children's heads turned slowly, eyes wide open, to gaze outside. It was just as Ava had remembered. Maybe, even worse. The old haunted-looking house still stood there leaning to one side. Bits of chipped paint hung loosely from the rotted wooden boards. Shutters shook violently in the breeze, being held by large and silky spider webs. Smoke still billowed from the crooked brick chimney, which was also falling apart. Tall dead grass and weeds covered the yard as a cool breeze swayed the few leaves that were left on the skeletal trees around the house. The woods in the background looked deeper, thicker, and darker than Ava had remembered. They cast a ghostly shadow over the house, and a light gray wispy fog seemed to unfold from the edges of the forest.

Charlotte squinted. "Why does she still have her Halloween decorations up?" she whispered.

"That's just the way her house looks," Ava answered, disturbed.

"But there are cobwebs hung all over the house," Nolan fussed. "You can't tell me she has that many spiders that live *on* her home that they were able to cover the whole thing in webs."

Charlotte gulped. A high-pitched howl echoed from inside the woods. All three kids jumped.

"What was that?" Nolan shrieked. "Was that a wolf?"

Dad laughed it off. "No, silly. It's probably just a coyote. They don't have wolves around here."

"What's a coyote?" Charlotte asked so quietly Ava could barely hear her.

"Well." Their dad scratched his head. "It's like a wild dog or a small wolf. They won't come inside the house or anything if that's what you're afraid of. They're probably just howling so they can find each other out here in the woods."

"Find each other?" Nolan asked in disbelief. "You mean there's more of them?"

Dad shrugged. "Maybe."

All three Alexander children sat back in their seats, eyes forward. Things were not looking good. And for some reason, their parents were completely fine with leaving them at this creepy old house in the middle of nowhere with coyotes howling all around it. Mom and Dad got out of the car and stretched. The kids didn't dare move. They shivered as more coyotes called out to each other.

A loud and eerie *CREAK* sounded outside the open van doors. The kids jerked in their seats and looked toward the sound. The front door of the house had opened, and several cats fled out of the doorway, *rawring* and *meowing* as they went. They were all black and short-haired with bright yellow eyes. One jumped onto the hood of the van and hissed at the children through the window. Nolan hissed back. Ava reached over and closed the van door, locking it.

THUD. THUD.

Something emerged from inside the house and now stood on the porch—a hefty woman dressed in a black blouse and skirt, a thick black and gray braid running down her back, with moles so large on her face, you could see them from the car. Ava could have sworn she even saw a hair in one.

The children all sucked in their breath. There stood their "baby-sitter" for the next week. In petrified unison, Ava, Nolan, and Charlotte whispered, "GROPPY."

3

The kids didn't move. Dad looked back at them from the gravel driveway and waved his hand in a motion that read *get out of the car*, but all three of the Alexander children shook their heads simultaneously. Mom smiled at Aunt Poppy like everything was normal, and walked briskly back to the van. She unlocked the car door nearest Ava and stuck her head in, eyeing all the kids individually. Ava could tell she wasn't happy.

"You're being very rude. Grab your suitcases and come say 'hello' to Aunt Poppy."

"She looks like a witch!" Nolan blurted out, then swiftly covered his mouth. Mom glared at Nolan, her nostrils slightly flared.

Oh no, Ava thought, *now she's really upset.*

"Her house looks scary," whispered Charlotte, still staring at the old shack covered in spiderwebs.

Mom let out a long sigh. "She's an old woman and she lives alone. She's not able to take care of everything around the house, that's all. The house is old, *not* scary, and she is *not* a witch, Nolan. I don't even know where you would get that idea." Nolan exhaled through his nose and rolled his eyes. "All of you better behave while you're here and thank Aunt Poppy for taking care of you. *We are grateful for her.*" She said the last sentence between clenched teeth.

The kids knew better than to push their mother any further, so they slowly undid their seat belts, slid out of the car, and grabbed their luggage from the trunk. Nolan pushed Ava to the front of the line, and they steadily plodded their way across the crunchy gravel behind their mom to the front steps where Groppy stood.

Ava reached the house first, head down. She hesitantly trudged up the steps, each step creaking louder than the last and stopped when she saw two pointed black shoes resting in front of her. Sitting slightly above the shoes were brightly striped purple and green socks.

"Poppy, you remember Ava, don't you? Ava, say 'hello' to Aunt Poppy," Mom said. Ava gulped and looked up at two mismatched green and blue eyes. Great-Aunt Poppy grinned a wide and crooked yellow grin. The smell of spices and herbs that floated off her clothes was unbelievable. Ava coughed and covered her mouth.

"Sorry," Ava wheezed as she coughed again, both embarrassed and frightened. Her mother looked concerned.

"I hope you're not getting sick, too." She felt Ava's forehead, then exhaled and relaxed. "Nope. You're good." *That's too bad,* Ava thought.

"Don't worry, dearie," said a scratchy, high-pitched voice. Groppy sounded like fingernails on a chalkboard. It made the hairs on Ava's neck stand up and she shivered. "I'll take good care of her. I have medicines, too, in case she gets sick." She looked down at Ava, smiling. "They're powerful. You'd feel better so quickly, you'd almost think it was . . . magic." She winked. Ava jerked her head toward her mom with a wild-eyed, frantic look. Mom looked unconcerned.

"Oh, just something from the drug store will be fine. We'll be back in a week to get the kids. They should be all right till then." Her mom smiled reassuringly. She looked back at the other two kids standing off in the yard. "Nolan! Charlotte! Come over here," she added more sweetly. The younger siblings slowly shuffled to the old porch, eyes fixed on Groppy.

"What beautiful children!" Groppy's voice pierced the air. Charlotte's hands flew up to cover her ears, a terrified and disturbed look on her face. "You look sweet enough to eat."

Nolan sucked in a breath after seeing the first close-up of Groppy's face and mouthed the word "MOLES" to his sisters. Mom shot him a look.

"We need to get going," Dad said, glancing at his watch. Mom looked lovingly at her children, leaning over and giving them all a huge hug. "I love you all so much! We'll be back before you know it. Be good to Aunt Poppy. Do as she asks. Okay?" The kids held on to her so tightly, she had to pry them off as she stood up. "Thank you again, Aunt Poppy."

"Anytime," Aunt Poppy replied, with a crooked grin. Ava, Nolan, and Charlotte gave their parents one last pleading look, but Mom only mouthed, "You'll be fine," and blew them a kiss.

They sank where they stood, defeated. Sadly they waved goodbye to their parents and watched them get in the car and drive away, leaving all three of them to survive a week here alone, out in the woods, with Groppy.

"Well, this will be fun. It's been a long time since I've had any visitors. Let me show you your rooms." Groppy held out an old, wrinkled hand covered in warts and guided the kids inside the crooked house. Nolan pushed on Ava's back and she stumbled into the threshold, jarring a large, black, hairy spider from its web that hung from the corner of the door frame. It fell in front of her face, wiggling and twitching. Ava screamed and covered her head with her arms. Groppy quickly reached out a hand and snatched the spider, holding it in her fist. The children eyed her in amazement.

"Go on," she said, never letting go of the huge spider. They all swiftly rushed into the house. A coyote howled. Groppy turned her head toward the woods. "I need to check on . . . something. Make yourselves at home," she called out to them from the front porch then slammed the door shut.

"Yeah right," Nolan muttered. "Like this place could feel like home."

"What did she do with the spider?" Charlotte asked.

"I don't know." Ava shuddered.

"I think she ate it," answered Nolan. They all froze as they entered the living room, mouths agape.

"It's just like I remembered," Ava breathed.

MEOW.

Each child jumped and saw nearly thirty black cats slinking toward them from the shadows, bright yellow eyes flashing. The cats came from all corners of the house, creeping down the stairs, sliding down curtains, and emerging from darkened doorways.

MEOW. MEOW. MEOW.

"Nice kitty," whispered Charlotte. "Sweet kitty?"

"How many cats does Groppy have?" Nolan asked slightly pan-icked as one started biting his shoelaces. Another latched onto his pants. He tried to swat them off, but another jumped up and dangled from his sweater. "Ahh! Ava, help me with these cats! Ava?"

Ava was staring at the walls, petrified, as all the brown and white owls stared menacingly back at her, watching. They grinned as if they could read her frightened thoughts.

MEOW! A cat flew from the air and landed on Ava's shoulder. She nearly fell backward as she pulled its claws from her shirt and ran to her siblings, tossing the cat on the ground with the hundreds of others. The Alexanders were now surrounded. The fluffy felines continued to push the kids deeper into a corner.

"What now?" Nolan desperately asked Ava. Ava was spooked, too, and she didn't know what to do. Being the oldest sibling, she stood in front of her brother and sister, protecting them from the mass of black fur and claws. The cats hissed and meowed as they crept closer. Their tails twitched. They looked ready to pounce.

"I saw a movie like this in kindergarten." Charlotte's voice shook. "It had these lions from the desert. They were chasing smaller animals, to eat them, and the lions would get the smaller animals trapped."

Ava looked around. They were surrounded. There was no way out.

"Like backed into a corner?" Nolan asked. Charlotte nodded. "The smaller animals were scared, but they thought they could get away by climbing. But then . . . " She paused. "They looked up."

"Charlotte," Ava asked softly, "what did the small animals see when they looked up?"

Charlotte whispered, "More lions."

Ava slowly turned her head toward the ceiling. Hundreds of bright yellow eyes glared at her from the railings of the balcony on the second floor. Their tails flicked in excitement. Nolan looked up, too, and whimpered.

"What happened next?" Ava asked, eyes fixed on the hundreds of black cats looming above her.

"I don't know." Trembling, Charlotte shook her head. "It was nap time and our teacher turned the movie off." She stared off into the distance. "But I couldn't sleep."

Thundering footsteps sounded from the hallway, making the children leap back deeper into the corner.

"Here, kitty kitty!" The crackling voice echoed throughout the house, calling the hoard of hungry cats. "Hereeee, kitty kitttyyyyy!"

Like statues, Ava, Nolan, and Charlotte watched in silence as all the hungry cats, sharp teeth bared, slowly turned their attention away from them and toward the awful crackling voice. They meowed and rawred, leaped, hissed, and ran away from the children toward Groppy. "Good kitties," Groppy cooed. "Precious kitties. I know you're hungry, but these children are not for *you* to eat."

"Did you hear that?" Nolan mouthed to Ava.

Charlotte's eyes were still as wide as saucers. Ava held a finger to her lips and motioned toward the end of the hallway. She got closer to her brother and shivering sister and whispered, "I think I remember a back door. We can sneak out of here and run to that last gas station to call Mom and Dad."

The others nodded in agreement. They had to get out of there. Sneaking past the mass of moving black fur, they quickly darted from the living room and down the adjoining hallway to the back door. Cats scurried under their feet, nearly tripping them at every step.

"There it is," Ava whispered in relief to her siblings. They reached the old wooden door, and Ava twisted the ancient bronze doorknob and pulled. It didn't budge. Maybe she needed to push it open. She gave it a hard shove. Still, the door didn't budge.

"Let me try," Nolan protested. He took a firm hold of the old knob with both hands and pulled as hard as he could. Still nothing, so he tried pushing as well.

"Is it locked?" asked Charlotte as she nervously danced on her tiptoes. Ava scanned the door. There wasn't a lock or a place for a key to go into. That was odd. Why wouldn't it open?

"We need to hurry." Ava panicked as she moved her brother aside. She gave the door another good push and pull.

"Children!" Groppy called from down the hall. "Where are you?" Ava could hear her own heart beating fiercely. It sounded like it would pop out of her chest.

Thud. Thud. Thud.

The footsteps came closer. "Children! Come out, come out, wher-ever you are!" Groppy's frightening voice carried down the hall. Nolan and Charlotte ducked behind Ava. The footsteps halted.

"Ahh! There you are!" Groppy peered down her long nose at the kids. "You know, it's not safe to go outside at night. *Especially* not here." As if trained, a coyote howled nearby from the woods, making Charlotte yelp. Groppy's mismatched eyes slanted and she gazed out-side. She quickly looked back at the kids.

"You must be so tired from your trip. Let me take you upstairs to your rooms." Again, she held her ghoul-like hand out for the children to follow. Nolan and Charlotte looked to Ava, but she was out of ideas. Her nod to Groppy was barely noticeable. Groppy grinned and led the kids back down the gloomy hall. Maybe the bedroom had a window they could climb out of and run away. Ava could always hope.

Groppy led them to the staircase. The owls from the portraits watched them all along the way. The stairs were old, wooden, and worn, like the rest of the house, and creaked sharply with every step. Up they went, following Groppy, to the second floor.

The sun was setting, and the house grew dark and more shadowed. Many cream-colored candles in brass holders that the children hadn't noticed before started popping up on walls and tables throughout the house, lit and flickering with tiny flames. They added an eerie glow to the already haunting decor.

Finally, they came to the balcony where all the cats had sat glaring at them just moments before and continued their procession down the hallway to an old red door with a shiny gold knob etched with flow-ers—poppies. Groppy reached for the handle, twisted, and pushed. This time the door opened, and cold air rushed out, along with a few cats. The door creaked as it slowly swayed open. The children leaned out from behind Groppy to peer inside. "Holy moly," whispered Nolan.

The walls were painted a vibrant purple and green in alternating stripes, just like Groppy's socks. The floor was covered with an inky black shag rug that reminded Ava of a black hole that might swallow them up if they stepped on it. On either side of the room sat two white wrought iron beds with deep crimson-red quilts. Many portraits hung on the wall, but they did not have owls in them. These portraits were filled with cats in human clothes, but to Ava's horror, their eyes also followed them around the room. There were cats in post carrier's uniforms, cat doctors, cat teachers, cat clowns, cat scientists, and cat astronauts. Charlotte giggled at the pictures. Nolan found them disturbing and wrinkled his nose. Groppy spoke and pointed to another red door on the right side of the room.

"That is a shared door. On the other side is your bedroom, Nolan." She smiled at him. "I thought you might like a room all to yourself. Alone. Away from your sisters."

Nolan did not like the sound of that, and he certainly did not want to be alone in this crazy house. "Oh, that's okay." He cleared his throat. "I . . . I can share a bed with Charlotte. She's small. Right, Charlotte? Didn't you want me to sleep with you?" Nolan stared wide-eyed at his little sister expectantly.

Charlotte looked up at Nolan with her big kitten eyes, innocently. "I did, but I kick in my sleep, remember? You wouldn't want to sleep with me. I'd keep you up all night." She smirked. "You can enjoy your bed. Alone."

Nolan sucked in a breath, shocked. Charlotte, trembling but triumphant, walked past him to her creepy iron bed and sat down. It squeaked liked hundreds of mice under her weight. She quickly got up and looked around for scurrying vermin. Nolan cautiously walked over to the red door and opened it to see his room. It was the same horrifyingly decorated room as his sister's room. At least it wasn't any creepier.

"The bathroom is down the hall," said Groppy. "Watch out for cats. Breakfast will be waiting for you in the morning." She paused and then added, "If I'm not here, don't be alarmed. I'll be back."

What's that supposed to mean? Ava wondered. *She'll be back? Where is she going?* Groppy thudded out the door and closed it but stopped a few inches before it shut, sticking her mole covered head back in. "Oh, and one more thing. Don't go up the stairs."

"You mean the ones we just went up?" Ava looked at both her siblings, confused. They shared the same look. "Or there's another floor to the house?" Ava asked. She was sure she had only seen one flight of stairs and this house only had two levels.

"Just don't go up the stairs!" Groppy croaked. And with that, she shut the door as her voice trailed off into the dark hallway.

4

IF THESE WALLS COULD TALK. NOLAN HAD HEARD THAT SAYING *MANY* times before from old people. Usually old people would say that right before telling him some incredibly long and boring story about the past.

Nolan had never really understood what that phrase meant, but lying there in that old iron bed by himself, with pictures of cats in clothes glaring at him while he stirred in his sheets, the walls *talked*. They mumbled and they moaned and made high-pitched sounds like a scream and low booming noises like thunder. As the wind howled outside, these old wooden walls spoke in sinister sounds from a haunted house, and Nolan did *not* like it. He pulled the sheets over his head and let out a shaky yawn. He was so tired, but there was no way he was sleeping tonight. Nolan turned on his side and stared out the only window he had in his room.

A large oak tree with long-reaching branches loomed across the smudged and dirty glass, casting shadows on the walls. The limbs looked like creepy arms reaching out to grab him. The wind howled outside, making the branches dance and the shadows jerk. He shivered and rolled over to look at the ceiling. "This place is a nightmare," he whispered to himself. *THUD.*

Nolan stilled in bed. What was that sound? He waited. "Ava?" he called out in a scared voice. No one answered. "Charlotte?" he breathed. "Is that you?" Still, no answer. Nolan could hear his heart beat faster in his chest. His imagination ran wild. Did a tree branch bump into the house? Did Groppy fall down the stairs? Was it a monster? Or maybe a zombie trying to break into the house and eat his brains. What was it?

Slowly and shakily, he peered over at the door. Maybe it had been his sisters, but no one was there. He firmly shut his eyes. If it wasn't his sisters, there was no telling what made that sound, and Nolan wasn't sure he wanted to know.

He took in a few deep breaths and lifted his head again, eyes still closed. He would look again on the count of three. *One . . . Two . . .* he paused, listening. *THREE.* Nolan's eyes opened wide and he quickly surveyed the dark room. He couldn't see anything.

SCRATCH. SCRATCH.

Nolan let out a sound like a whimper. What was that? There was only one place he hadn't checked—under the bed. He shook his head. There was no way he was looking down there. He pulled the sheets back over his head and curled into a tight ball. *SCRATCH. SCRATCH. SCRATCH.*

Nolan plugged his ears. If he ignored it, it would go away. He had used the same tactic on his little sister, and it had almost always worked. *SCRATCH. SCRATCH.* He pulled his body closer, hugged his knees, and tried to force himself to fall asleep. *SCRATCH.*

Whatever was making that noise was not going to go away, no matter how much Nolan wished it would. He had to do something. "You have to be brave," he whispered to himself completely unconvinced. "You . . . you can do this." He started to unfold from his curled-up position. "You *are* brave." Nolan's voice grew more confident. He was now sitting up in bed, but his eyes were closed again. He took a deep breath and exhaled, then looked out. A dark shape sat perched outside the window.

Nolan yelped and quickly covered his face with the covers. He hadn't expected to actually see something. But there it was! Outside the window. He waited. Nothing happened. He peeked out from behind the sheets. The creature was still sitting there on the windowsill. Curious, Nolan stared at it.

It wasn't a large shape. Did it look furry? The monster reached out a sinister limb and slid its slim arm down the window. *SCRATCH.* "Wait a minute," Nolan whispered. He felt courage pulse through his veins and squinted to peer more closely at the shape. Then he recognized what it was, and his eyes rolled with an exasperated sigh. "Good grief. It's a cat."

Nolan groaned and threw the sheets off, angrily plopped off the bed, and shuffled over to the window. "I can't believe I was terrified of one of Groppy's dumb ole cats." They weren't so scary when there was only one and not a thousand coming at him all at once. Still, he quickly glanced outside to make sure no others were waiting to attack him from the tree. No, just the one cat.

Nolan placed his hands on his hips and stared out at the black feline perched on the windowsill. It glared back with its hazel eyes, which Nolan found interesting because all the other cats' eyes were yellow. "I don't have any food if that's what you want," he told the cat blankly. Nolan's stomach grumbled at the thought of food. He rubbed his belly. Gosh, he was hungry.

"Meow," said the cat. Nolan looked back at the small animal and his eyebrows furrowed. "MEOW." The cat swatted at the window with its paw. Its tail flicked back and forth in an agitated manner.

"What?" replied Nolan, equally agitated. "Do you want back in the house?"

The cat blinked and glared back with enlarged pupils. "Well, that would be nice, yes."

Nolan's mouth dropped and he took a step back from the window. Did that cat just talk?

5

THE CAT STARED AT NOLAN THROUGH THE WINDOW, THEN PROceeded to lick its paw and rub its ears.

"Did you . . . ?" Nolan couldn't find the words. Or he could, but this was insane. Or he was. "Did you just talk?" The cat purred and rubbed up against the window. "No, cats can't talk. I'm just going loopy in this creepy house." He rubbed his tired, red eyes and groaned. "I need some sleep."

"I don't care what *you* need. *I need* back in the house. So, open the window."

Nolan put his hands to his mouth in shock, then lowered them back down. He wasn't going crazy after all.

"So, you *can* talk?"

"Yes, but it doesn't appear that you understand. Let me IN."

For a talking cat, this one was kind of rude. But then, weren't all cats rude? Nolan pushed that thought aside and shakily turned the old rusted lock on the window and pried it open. There was a *CREAK*, followed by a lot of dust and a few spiders scurrying back outside. Once the window was fully opened, the cat gracefully leaped onto the floor, waltzed over to the bed, and jumped onto the mattress. It arched its back, stretching, and dug its claws into the sheets.

"Umm." Nolan pointed. "That's *my* bed." He could not believe he was talking to a cat that could understand him.

"I know." The cat yawned and curled up in the sheets, taking up the middle of the bed. "But this is *much* more comfortable than a tree limb."

Nolan was so stunned by the talking cat that he didn't care that it was shedding fur all over his sheets. Well, maybe he cared a little.

Nolan closed the window and locked it tight just in case there was anything else out there that wanted inside. He walked over to the cat and gingerly sat down beside it. He didn't want it to run away. Even though it was a talking cat, it had helped Nolan forget how freaked out he was about the spooky house and Groppy. Nolan flicked some cat hair off the sheets. "My name is Nolan. Do you have a name?"

The cat stopped licking its leg to look up at Nolan, its tongue still sticking out, making Nolan snicker. The feline curled its lip, showing one of its fangs. Nolan immediately stopped laughing.

"Yes, I do," the cat answered. It then went back to grooming its fur.

Nolan tried to wait patiently, but he was just a nine-year-old kid, and kids aren't known for their patience. "Well, then what is it?"

"What is what?" said the cat as he yawned making Nolan yawn, too.

"Your name?" Nolan spat impatiently.

"Well, there is no need to get snippy," the cat hissed back. "You only asked if I had a name. You didn't ask what it was. You will learn that around here, if you want something, you must be very careful with your choice of words. Try again."

Nolan wasn't sure what that meant. He was starting to get hangry from lack of food, but he rolled his eyes and sighed just the same. "What is your name?" he asked the cat.

"Merlin."

Nolan leaned back and scratched his head. "Merlin? Like the wizard from King Arthur stories?"

"Yes." Merlin twitched his tail. "Like the wizard from those stories." Nolan opened his mouth to ask another question, but Merlin interjected. "No. I am not that wizard, so don't bother asking." That was a huge bummer. But still, a talking cat. How awesome was this? Maybe Nolan could survive this week at Groppy's after all. His stomach let out another long growl.

"I'll never be able to sleep with your stomach making all that noise," Merlin said apathetically. "Why don't you eat something? That way, I can sleep."

Nolan shrugged. "I don't know where the food is, and there is no way I'm walking through this house alone at night. Besides, it's probably all gross-looking vegetables or green slime or something."

"Well, then, wish for what you want," Merlin said matter-of-factly.

"What?" Nolan scrunched his nose. "How would that work?"

"You just say *I wish*, state the food that you want, and then wait till it comes out of the large pot."

Nolan looked around the room. "What large pot?"

"It's not in here." Merlin flexed his claws, digging them into the sheets. "It's in her secret room where she keeps all the smelly spices and herbs and other things."

That got Nolan's attention. He leaned in closer to Merlin and whispered, "Is it up the stairs?"

The cat blinked, his bright hazel eyes shining in the darkness. "Did you brush your teeth today?" Merlin gagged. Nolan licked his teeth with his tongue. He might have forgotten to do that. The cat coughed and cleared his throat. "To answer your question, yes."

Now Nolan was excited, but he made sure to back away from Merlin before asking the next question. "Where are the stairs?"

The ebony cat motioned with one of his paws toward the bedroom door. "Go through any red door. It will take you there." He turned away from Nolan and curled into a tight circle, purring contently. Nolan looked at the door left ajar, completely confused, and then turned back to Merlin.

"But that door just goes to my sister's room. There's no large pot or spices in there. Just two beds, a rug, and some weird cat portraits."

Merlin let out a small growl. "You have to close the door and open it from the right side."

That confused Nolan more. "Like the correct side? Not the wrong side, but the right side?"

The cat's tail whipped back and forth. "No! Look." Merlin jumped off the bed and lumbered over to the door. He pointed with his tail. "This doorknob is on the left side of the door, yes?"

Nolan shrugged. "Yea, I can see that."

Merlin continued. "This opens the door into the bedroom. But if you were to move the doorknob to the right side of the door and open it from the right, the room changes."

"That's impossible," Nolan scoffed. Of course, he was hearing this from a talking cat, so maybe it wasn't *completely* impossible. Still.

Merlin growled again. "Fine. Have it your way and stay hungry." He walked back over to the bed and hopped in, snuggling up against the warm comforter. Nolan scratched his head.

"I'm sorry, it's just, you can't just remove a doorknob. They're screwed in or something, and if I were to open the door with the knob on the right side, it would still be my sister's bedroom." Merlin ignored Nolan and purred deeply. This only annoyed Nolan and he let out a heavy sigh. "This is ridiculous. I'm awake in the middle of the night talking to a cat and he says I can get food if I change the doorknob."

"And say *I wish*," Merlin added.

"Right," Nolan nodded sarcastically, "And say *I wish* into a large pot."

GRUMBLE.

This time the noise was Nolan's stomach. He was *beyond* hungry. Nolan looked over at the door, questioning it. He knew nothing would happen, but his feet touched the floor and he found himself walking to the red door and reaching out for the golden knob. He stopped. "Is this crazy? Or am I just really hungry and going crazy?"

"Yes, to all," Merlin shot back from the bed. "Now go eat and leave me alone to sleep."

Wow. This cat had a grumpy attitude. Nolan shrugged and took hold of the doorknob and closed the door. The latch clicked in place. "Okay, so now I just . . . " He gave a doubtful tug at the doorknob. To his complete astonishment, it came out of the door and the hole closed in as if it was never there. "What in the world?" Nolan gasped.

He looked over to the right side of the door, and another hole magically appeared for the golden knob to be placed into. An enthusiastic grin spread across his face. He placed the knob in the hole and heard a resounding *CLICK* as it fit perfectly in place. Nolan's heart quickened in excitement. Could this really be happening? Hands trembling, Nolan turned the knob and slowly pushed the door ajar. His jaw dropped.

What lay in front of Nolan was not his sisters' bedroom, but a dark, winding, ancient wooden staircase lit by waxy, dripping, flickering candles that hung along the walls. "Holy moly," Nolan breathed.

It was in fact the stairs going up, the ones Groppy *specifically* said to stay away from. He knew it had to be them. Nolan hesitated outside the door frame. Should he go? Merlin had said there was food up there, and he was *really* hungry. But what else was hidden up there? What was Groppy hiding? Was it good? Was it scary? Maybe he should wake his sisters. But no, they would never believe him. Especially Ava. Not when he got the idea from a talking cat. Besides, once he showed her, she would probably ruin the fun and tell him he couldn't go up the stairs.

Nolan exhaled. He'd made up his mind. With determination, he took one step inside the stairwell and the red door closed behind him with a soft *CLICK*.

* * *

In the adjacent bedroom, Ava was staring at the ceiling, red, exhausted eyes wide awake. She had sat on the edge of Charlotte's bed until her little sister finally fell asleep. Then she dragged her tired feet over to her bed and plopped down on her back.

Charlotte had asked for a bedtime story, and Ava tried to make it a very happy one. It had been a silly story about a unicorn that liked to eat buttercups and fly around rainbows, but Ava knew her sister liked that kind of stuff. She was only six.

Charlotte eventually fell asleep listening to Ava's calm and familiar voice. But now that Charlotte was asleep and Ava wasn't hearing herself talk, all she heard were the scary and ominous noises that came from deep within the house.

HISS. MUMBLE. SCREECH. BOOM. THUD. SCRATCH. SCRATCH. GRUMBLE.

I just have to keep us alive for the week, she thought. She turned on her side and listened to the wind whirl outside her window while a portrait of a cat in business clothes stared back at her from the green and purple striped wall. She had tried opening the window before they went to bed, but the window would not budge.

Tomorrow would be a new day, and Ava was sure she could keep them all alive for just a few more days till their parents came back.

CLICK.

What made that sound? Ava picked her head up off the bed and peered over at her sister. "Charlotte?" she whispered. Charlotte didn't answer back. All Ava heard was her sister's deep breathing as she peacefully slept. *Well, that makes one of us,* she thought. She looked over at the door connecting them to Nolan's room. It was closed. *Huh. I thought he left that open.*

"Nolan," Ava whispered. No one answered. "NOLAN," she said louder. Why would he close the door? Ava looked around the room cautiously, then slid off her bed and quietly tip-toed over to the red door. She looked back at Charlotte still fast asleep and grabbed hold of the doorknob and turned it. Slowly the door opened into her brother's bedroom. Ava looked around. All appeared to be normal. Well, ugly and scary *normal.* "I guess it was nothing."

Ava turned to leave but then glanced over at Nolan's bed. She froze. Nolan was not in his bed. Instead, curled up in the sheets, was a peacefully sleeping black cat.

Nolan was gone.

6

"This *might* have been a bad idea," Nolan muttered to himself as he slowly crept up the wooden staircase. The combination of constant winding steps and his growing hunger pains made Nolan sick to his stomach. He thought he might even vomit. Nolan put a hand to his mouth and his belly. "Good grief. How many steps are there?" Wax trickled off the candles and splat across the old stairs as he steadily moved upward, always on the lookout for big dangling spiders, crazy cats, or worse, old smelly Groppy.

Exhaustion growing, he finally leaned against a wall and rubbed his eyes. "Why in the world did I listen to a cat?" Nolan was starting to think Merlin had lied to him when he glanced up and saw another red door just a few steps away. "Hallelujah! I've made it! Food, here I come." His fists pumped into the air, and he quickly jumped up the last few steps. With the promise of food nearby, Nolan could find enough energy to do just about anything.

The door was like the one in his bedroom, but he eyed it carefully, just in case it was booby-trapped. Reaching out a timid finger, he lightly touched the doorknob. Nothing happened. Nolan shrugged and twisted the golden knob, giving the door a shove. Immediately, an overpowering smell of herbs, spices, and who-knows-what slapped Nolan in the face and his eyes watered.

"Holy moly." He coughed. "It smells like Groppy in here." He covered his nose and mouth with his t-shirt and bravely walked in.

Candles flickered around the dark room. There were bookcases along one wall filled with old -looking and worn-out books with deep, colorful spines of reds, blues, and greens, traced over with gold and silver trim. Many of the books were completely covered in a thick layer of dust that made Nolan sneeze violently as he walked by. A dust cloud erupted from the shelves. He gagged, waved it away, and moved to the opposite wall. It was lined with shelves and shelves of glass vials and containers. "Interesting. This must be where she keeps her spices. I guess Groppy likes to cook. Or maybe, make her potions?"

Nolan mused over the different containers and their contents. Most of the containers were round cylinders with a cork stopper on the top. Quite a few were square, some rectangular, and a small number were in the shape of a star. The glasses were all different colors, and the contents inside looked either dry like dirt or wet like water. Nolan leaned in closer to one shelf full of liquid vials but quickly jumped back when an eyeball from one of the glasses stared up at him. "Whoa, cool." He took a timid step closer and noticed other squiggly objects in the bottles right beside the wet eyeball. "*What* are you up to, Groppy?" Nolan said as he reached out a brave finger and touched a few containers. He poked one with wriggly lizard tails a little too hard, and it rocked off the shelf. Luckily, he grabbed it right before it hit the floor. "That was close," he breathed.

A large wooden table stood in the middle of the room. Arranged on it were a few vials, small containers, and an old black book. Nolan walked over and peered at the book cover. The title, in shiny gold letters, read the word "Grimoire." Nolan tried to sound it out. "Grimore. Grim-moreey. Grim-moi-ray?" Nolan shrugged since he really didn't care about the pronunciation and quickly noticed there was a bookmark in one of the pages. He looked around to make sure that no one was watching and slid a finger in between the thick pages of the book, then swiftly flipped it open. It opened to a yellowed page titled "Wishing Spell." Nolan's eyes lit up with wonder and curiosity and he quickly kept reading.

A spell for your deepest desires, fantastical dreams, or darkest wishes . . . That last part gave Nolan the willies. "Well, my deepest desire right now is a grilled cheese sandwich. I don't consider that a dark wish." He continued. *Ingredients: Eye of Brown Toad, Fairy Dander, Pinch of Witch Hazel, Pixie House Dust, Tail of Newt, Blood of Black Widow Spider, Pond Water, Hair of a Unicorn, a Batwing, and Honey.* Nolan's nose twitched as he read the ingredients. "This sounds super nasty. Is she eating this stuff?"

Mix all ingredients in a cast-iron cauldron over medium-low heat for 6 hours. When the bubbling stops, the potion is ready. Remember: Be careful what you wish for.

"That's it? You just wish on it? At least you don't have to drink it."

Nolan looked toward the end of the room where a fireplace sat. Hanging above the dying flames was a small cauldron. "I wonder . . . " He rubbed his chin. *Maybe this is the wishing potion Merlin was talking about.* Nolan glanced down at the vials scattered on the table: Hair of a Unicorn, Eye of Brown Toad, Blood of Black Widow Spider, Fairy Dander, Pond Water, Pixie House Dust, a Batwing, Tail of Newt, Honey; these were all ingredients for a Wishing Potion. Nolan grinned. If Ava had been here, she would definitely tell him this was a bad idea. He chuckled to himself. Good thing she wasn't here.

Nolan walked over to the black pot in the fireplace. He peered inside to see a murky-looking liquid with no bubbles. It smelled like rotten eggs *and* roses. He straightened up quickly. "Yikes, that is some *stinky* stuff. What did Merlin say? You had to start the sentence with *I wish.*"

Nolan exhaled. He could feel the hairs on the back of his neck start to stand. There was no telling what was going to happen. "Here goes nothing," he whispered. "I wish . . . " He squeaked and cleared his throat. "I wish . . . for . . . " He glanced around again, making sure no one was there then stared back at the pot. "A grilled cheese sandwich." Rumbling immediately erupted from within the cauldron. Nolan jumped back. A bright and sparkling light shone out from the murky purple liquid and some *thing* started to slowly rise from the gooey liquid within the cauldron. Nolan's mouth dropped and his eyes lit up. "Holy moly."

7

NOLAN COULDN'T BELIEVE WHAT HE WAS SEEING. RIGHT IN FRONT OF him, floating above the cauldron, was a perfectly made grilled cheese sandwich.

In amazement, he extended his fingers toward the floating cheesy goodness. He could feel the heat coming from the grilled bread. His mouth began to water. Carefully, he reached around the floating sandwich with both hands and snatched it midair, bringing it close to his face. He breathed in. Oh yeah, this was a grilled cheese sandwich. He took another whiff. Cheddar cheese. Not that nasty kind that tasted like Play-Doh. Too many times he had unfortunately gobbled that gross cheese up at the baby showers his mom dragged him to. He quickly learned it is always best to sniff cheese, then eat.

Completely forgetting that the sandwich came from a pot of smelly water, Nolan opened his mouth wide and took a huge bite. The gooey cheese stretched from his lips to the sandwich. "Where have you been all my life?" he mumbled while chomping into the crunchy buttered bread.

After he finished that sandwich, he wished for another sandwich, because, why not? Once his belly was satisfied, he decided it was time to head back to his room. He would sleep well tonight now that he had a full stomach. Nolan *had* to tell his sisters about this magical pot that granted wishes. They were going to *flip out*. What fun could they get into this week?

As he headed back down the creaky staircase, his mind raced with ideas of all the things they could wish for. They could wish for more food, like cheeseburgers, French fries, chocolate cake, cookie dough, and ice cream. That way they wouldn't have to eat whatever nasty thing Groppy made. Or they could wish for video games, a huge TV— since he noticed Groppy *didn't* have one—he should probably wish for Wi-Fi as well, along with a remote-control car, or an actual car! Make it an *invisible* car. They technically weren't old enough to drive, but it would still be cool to have one. The options were *literally* endless.

Nolan giddily thought about all these wishes, but something unsettling started to scratch at the back of his mind. Something was wrong. He knew it took him forever to get up these stairs, but shouldn't he have already gotten to the bedroom door by now? He tried not to let it bother him and picked up the pace as he ran down more stairs. They just kept winding and winding and winding, but no door was in sight. Just more stairs. Nolan started to panic, and his heart raced. "Where's the red door?"

* * *

Ava rubbed her eyes with the palms of her hands, frustrated. Why couldn't Nolan just stay in his room? She didn't want to look for him in this spooky house. It was difficult enough being the oldest and having to watch out for siblings. It was even more difficult to pretend like she was brave when she was, honestly, really scared. And where in the world had this cat come from on Nolan's bed? The doors and windows were shut. Maybe it had been hiding under the bed? Or, wait. Maybe it was . . . "Nolan?" Ava whispered to the cat. The feline continued to sleep. No, that was a crazy thought. The cat was not Nolan.

Ava huffed and headed back to her and Charlotte's room, closing the red door to Nolan's bedroom behind her. She sat on her bed and exhaled deeply. What was she going to do? They hadn't even been here one day, and she had lost her brother.

SLAM. Ava bolted from the bed. A door had been shut. Slammed shut. Ava jerked her head toward the sound. It was Nolan's bedroom door. But it was already closed. You can't re-close a closed door. She raced toward it and yanked it open. Nolan was standing there in his room, gasping for air. His shirt was covered in food stains, and he had crumbs near his mouth and greasy-looking fingers. Drops of sweat gathered on his forehead. His hair was frazzled and sticking out in all directions.

"Nolan!" Ava shouted bewildered. "Where on earth have you been? And why . . . " She sniffed the air. "Why do you smell like cheese?" Nolan tried to explain but couldn't talk for his heavy breathing. Ava was now even more confused. "And why are you panting and out of breath?" He held up a hand to let her know he needed a minute and collapsed on the bed by the slumbering cat.

Merlin slept through all of this, but Charlotte did not. All the noise of slamming doors and Ava's questions woke her instantly, and Charlotte opened her eyes to a dark and empty bedroom. She was all alone. Except for the cat portraits that stared at her from the walls. Tears welled in Charlotte's eyes, and the moment she heard her sister's voice in the next room, she ran toward it, frightened. "Ava!" she cried. She ran to Ava's side and latched on, giving her a bear hug. Her big sister instinctively reached a hand down to calm Charlotte. Ava was still bewildered as to why Nolan was exhausted and smelled like cheese.

Charlotte's terrified yelling woke up Merlin. He was not pleased. The cat yawned and looked around, most annoyed. A tall girl was shouting at Nolan, a smaller girl was attached to her side, crying, and Nolan was panting like he had just run a marathon. This was too much for Merlin to handle.

"Everyone, quiet!" Merlin hissed. That did it. Ava's questions ceased and Charlotte's sniffles stopped instantly. They stared blankly at the black cat. "Finally." Merlin stretched. "It sounded like a circus in here. Do you have any idea how late it is? So rude." Ava gaped at Merlin, then to Nolan, then back to Merlin. Nolan had now finally regained his breath and pointed a greasy finger at the cat.

"Ava this is Merlin. Charlotte, Merlin. He's a . . . *talking* cat. I didn't think you would believe me, so I didn't tell you." Ava continued to stare at Nolan in astonishment. "Oh, and that door is magical." He nodded to his bedroom door. "I found the stairs that go up that Groppy told us *not* to go to and wished for a grilled cheese sandwich from a magic cauldron filled with dirty, smelly water. Actually, I wished for two sandwiches. They were really good, and I was *starving*."

Charlotte eyed Merlin with wonder. Ava finally regained her ability to talk, and her hands shifted to her hips as she stood over her brother.

"That cat . . . can talk? And what? A magic door? Dirty cauldron?" She could not believe what she was hearing. Except for the part about the talking cat. That was obviously true.

Nolan nodded. "Yes. Cat talks. Magic door. Magic dirty water in big pot." Ava slowly shook her head. This was nuts.

Charlotte gently let go of her sister's leg and carefully tip-toed over to Merlin, who eyed her suspiciously from the bed. She crouched down in front of him and held out a small hand. "Hi, Merlin kitty," she said softly. She waited for Merlin to lean into her palm. He stared her down. Little humans looked cute, but they were not harmless and usually petted fur the *wrong* way and pulled cat's tails. Merlin sniffed the air around Charlotte's hand. She smelled like strawberries. He liked that. The cat slowly moved the top of his head toward her outstretched fingers and allowed her to pet him. Charlotte petted him and scratched his head. Merlin purred loudly and happily.

Ava was still trying to wrap her head around everything. "Where did you go, Nolan?"

"I told you! The magic door took me to Groppy's secret potion room." Nolan shrugged. "I know. It's bonkers, but it's true."

"Ha! Yeah, it's bonkers, all right." Ava crossed her arms.

"Oh, and there's one more thing," Nolan added hesitantly.

"What?" Ava half-laughed, throwing her hands up. "Are you *now* going to tell me our great-aunt is *actually* a witch?" Nolan said nothing and Ava's smile dropped. "Nolan?" She asked hesitantly.

"Not *actually*," his eyes widened as he nodded. "Definitely. Groppy is *definitely* a witch and her magic is *very* real."

This time it was Ava who said, "Holy moly."

8

NOLAN SLOWLY CLOSED HIS BEDROOM DOOR AND REPLICATED THE actions he had done an hour before, revealing the stairs to his sisters. Ava had her doubts up until she saw the old staircase appear out of nowhere. And while she was shocked and a bit terrified, she was also a little pleased. She always thought Groppy might be a witch, but her parents had never believed her. This magic door proved she had been right all along. Just wait till she told Mom about this.

"Come on!" Nolan motioned toward them excitedly. "I can take you to Groppy's spell room. It's so cool!" Nolan walked through the door frame, but a firm hand grabbed him by the wrist and pulled him back. He turned, annoyed, and saw Ava shaking her head with a perturbed look on her face.

"Nolan, it was *extremely* irresponsible for you to go by yourself the first time and risk getting caught. It would be *even* dumber to go a second time and expect to *not* get caught. Not to mention the fact that Groppy *specifically* told us not to go up the stairs. These are obviously those stairs. And on the *very* night she tells us to stay away from them, you find them and go up anyway."

Nolan exhaled and rolled his eyes. Were his actions irresponsible? Yes. But, typical Nolan? Also, yes. Even so, Ava *was* curious to see this magical room, but she had to play it cool. She needed to be responsible, after all, because apparently, Nolan was not. Charlotte was not nearly as excited about the staircase as Ava was. She was too caught up in talking with Merlin and petting his soft and fluffy fur.

"Okay." Ava nodded. "I think it would be best if we went back to bed."

"But . . . " Nolan protested. Ava held her hand up.

"You didn't let me finish. We go back to bed and tomorrow, when Groppy is out of the house"—Ava added hesitantly—"we go up the stairs." Nolan clapped his hands together and smiled. This idea seemed more responsible to Ava. Groppy had mentioned she might not be there for breakfast, which Ava still thought was odd, but then Groppy was an odd person.

So, they all went back to bed, waiting for the adventure the next day held. Sleep came much easier now. Fear had been replaced by excitement, magic, and mystery. Nolan could sleep since he had a full stomach. Charlotte had nothing to be afraid of now that she had a talking cat asleep at the foot of her bed. And Ava, knowing that everyone was in their beds, and being exhausted from being the "adult" of the group, drifted off to sleep and dreamed odd dreams with creepy painted walls, glaring eyes, talking cats, and Groppy casting spells.

* * *

A strange smell drifted into Ava's nose and jerked her awake. She rubbed her eyes and noticed it was morning. The sun shone through the dusty windows and onto the black hole shag rug that was now visibly covered in black cat hair. In fact, the rug's original color might not have even been black. Ava shuddered and quickly darted her eyes to Charlotte's bed and Nolan's in the other room. Good. Both were still in bed and asleep. They had made it through the first night. Today marked day two of survival and the first full day at Groppy's.

Ava sniffed the air. What in the world was that? Was that breakfast? Her nose wrinkled as she breathed in the unappealing smell.

"Charlotte," Ava said softly, "wake up."

"Hmm?" Charlotte answered, half awake. Ava smiled and pushed off her red sheets and slid off the bed with a loud *SCREECH*. She softly padded to Nolan's room. After his adventure last night, she had made sure he left his door wide open.

"Nolan, come on. It's time to get up."

"Go away," Nolan grumbled and pulled the sheets up over his head. Ava sighed and walked over, pulling the sheets back down. The sun's bright rays coming in from the window hit Nolan square in the face. *HISSSS*. Nolan grabbed the pillow from behind his head and covered his eyes. Ava laughed.

"You know, last night, I thought you had turned into a cat. Now, I'm not so sure you didn't." She chuckled.

"Why does the sun have to be so *stinking* bright in the morning?" came Nolan's muffled response from behind the pillow.

"Because it's the only way to wake us up, I guess." Ava shrugged. "Come on, we need to see what Groppy made for breakfast."

Nolan sniffed the air. "I think I'll pass," he answered and turned on his side. Ava shook her head and went back to Charlotte. She was sitting up in bed and stroking Merlin, telling him about her dreams. Merlin didn't seem to mind the extra attention. It appeared he was somewhat enjoying the story of a unicorn eating a rainbow that tasted of jelly beans, and then later, pooping jelly beans. As Charlotte finished her story, Nolan finally shuffled into the room, a blanket wrapped around his body. "Let's get this over with."

The three kids and the cat traveled back down the stairs. The house wasn't as scary-looking in the day as it had been at night. Now, it just looked like an old, dusty, and weirdly decorated house. The children followed the odd smell downstairs, dodging random cobwebs and cats along the way to the kitchen.

Groppy's kitchen looked almost like a *normal* kitchen. It had brown, crooked cabinets, a small fridge, and a large, deep sink, but the stove was weird looking. It was rectangular and black; a fire was burning inside and there was a large pipe coming out from the middle of it and disappearing into the ceiling. "It's a wood-burning stove," said Merlin when he noticed the kid's confused-looking faces. They would have to take his word for it. On top of the stove sat a large pot that was bubbling.

"Look," said Charlotte. She pointed to the table. There was a letter written in scribbly handwriting addressed to "Children."

Ava reached out for it, but Nolan swiftly grabbed the letter before she could and read through it. "Groppy is gone!" he sang as he threw the letter down. "So, let's go up the secret stairs and not eat this gross food."

"Don't move," Ava ordered. Nolan halted and grumbled while she picked up the letter herself and read it.

Children, sorry to fly, but something has come up that I need to take care of. I conjured you some breakfast. Eat it quick before it hardens. I'll be back before the spiders come out.
—Aunt Poppy

P.S. Don't go up the stairs.
P.S.S. Don't go outside.

Something was very wrong here, and Ava didn't like it. Charlotte pulled up a stool to get a better look at what was in the pot. "Ew!" she shrieked. "What is that stuff?" Merlin jumped onto the counter to peer inside and smell the bubbling crude.

"Porridge," he said disgustedly. "Prune porridge. Her typical breakfast."

"Prunes?" Charlotte wrinkled her nose. "What are those?"

"It's a dried-out plum," Ava answered, still looking over the letter.

"They smell yucky." Charlotte leaned back over the pot. "Why would anyone eat this?"

"To help them go number two," Nolan said, scratching and sniffing an old stain on his shirt. Charlotte looked up, confused. Nolan further explained. "Remember that time I ate the two blocks of cheese Dad had bought to make homemade pizza?" Charlotte nodded. "Well, it stopped me up, bad. I couldn't poop for a week, so Mom made me drink some prune juice. That stuff was *nasty*. But it worked. I was on the toilet pretty much for the rest of the day. Read through a lot of comics." Nolan shuddered, remembering the experience. "I thought that porridge smelled familiar. You think it smells bad. Just wait till you taste it. Yuck city. Groppy must be stopped up pretty bad."

"Nolan," Ava warned, grossed out.

"What?" He shrugged. "It's true."

Charlotte's bottom lip quivered. "But . . . but I don't want to eat that. I don't want to poop a lot."

"And you're not," Nolan answered matter-of-factly. "Because we're going up the forbidden stairs and getting some cereal, blueberry pancakes, or McDonald's. Something that isn't made of prunes."

Charlotte grinned. "We are?" she whispered excitedly.

"Yes," Nolan answered triumphantly, but still glanced over at Ava as he punched a fist into the air. "To the forbidden stairs!"

"Just hold your horses," Ava interrupted.

"Geez," Nolan whined. "Why do you always have to be such a party pooper?"

Ava gestured to the pot. "Groppy made us this . . . stuff. We can't just leave it here."

Nolan glanced over at the stove and shrugged. "Sure, we can." And before Ava could protest, he grabbed Charlotte's hand and whisked her out of the kitchen and back up the stairs to their rooms, Charlotte giggling all the way.

Ava turned to Merlin, frustrated. "They don't listen to me."

Merlin licked his paw, disinterested. "When do children ever like listening to adults?" he answered her blankly. Ava frowned. Merlin jumped to the kitchen table and sat down near her. "But you aren't an adult, are you?" He looked at her and tilted his head. "Aren't you still a kid?"

Hmm. Ava hadn't really thought about that. She was eleven and a half. Next year she would turn twelve. She was almost a preteen. Nearly an adult. But then, she had always acted old for her age. She couldn't help it. She liked to take charge. Her mouth twisted. "I guess, technically, I'm still a kid."

"Well, then enjoy it. You're only a kid once. Time is something that crawls by when you're young but flies away when you're old. Nobody ever wishes for less time."

This was the first time Ava had received advice from a cat, and she had to admit, it was pretty good. Well, maybe just this once, she could have some fun. She looked pleased with her decision but turned back to the stove. "But what about the porridge?"

Merlin flicked his tail. "Eh, maybe the cats will eat it."

"Would you?" She raised her eyebrows.

Merlin hissed. "Gracious, no. That stuff is dreadful. But what do the cats know about good taste? They're just cats."

Ava smiled. "Well, let's head upstairs, then." But, before they left, Ava did at least make sure the fire was out in the stove. As for the porridge, she hoped it would just magically disappear.

9

When Ava reached Nolan's bedroom, she found him and Charlotte sitting on the bed, elbows on their knees, heads rested in their hands. They perked up as she walked through the door.

"You came!" Charlotte beamed happily.

"I knew she would," Nolan prodded. Ava rolled her eyes.

"Yes, I'm here. So, what are we waiting for?" Nolan quickly jumped off the bed and closed the door behind Ava. Both girls watched in anticipation as he changed the doorknob from the left side to the right and opened the door. There, just like the night before, was the eerie staircase. Nolan turned to his sisters and smiled. "Ready to make some wishes?"

* * *

They traveled up the old staircase completely mystified. The candles' small flames flickered and cast the group's shadows on the wall. Merlin had decided to join them as well, and he padded along beside Charlotte.

"Just a few more steps," Nolan said, turning back to the others.

"How long is this staircase?" Ava asked.

"I'm not sure," replied Nolan as he continued the climb. "Last night, it seemed to last forever, but then, coming down was even longer. I didn't think I would ever find the door back."

Ava halted. "What do you mean you didn't know if you could *find* the door back?"

"Uhhh. The door kind of disappeared," Nolan mumbled.

Ava's eyes widened. "It did what? You mean we could get stuck in this stairwell?" Ava didn't like to admit it, but she was claustrophobic and did *not* like the idea of being stuck in a narrow, winding, creepy staircase with spiders for the rest of her life.

"But the door came back! I must have miscounted steps or something. We're fine. I think . . . " Nolan was not reassuring.

Merlin interrupted. "You cannot reenter an open door."

Nolan and Ava turned to look down at the cat.

"What do you mean?" Ava questioned.

"I mean," continued Merlin, "that the door you enter must remain shut for you to return."

"That is incredibly . . . confusing," Nolan said as he rubbed his temples. "Are you talking about the bedroom door?" Merlin nodded in reply. Ava snapped her fingers.

"Oh! I understand. Last night when I heard your door close the first time, I went in to check on you and couldn't find you. I just sat on your bed for the longest time with your door *open* so I could keep an eye on Charlotte in her bed. The moment I returned to my room and *closed* your door, I heard it slam shut, again, once I was back on my bed. You weren't able to return because I had your bedroom door open."

"The door did seem to pop up out of nowhere," Nolan pondered.

"Wait. How do we make sure the door stays shut so *we* can return?" Ava frantically asked Merlin.

"Well, typically there is no one in the house other than Groppy, and the cats can't open the door with their paws, so you should be fine." Merlin didn't seem to be taking this seriously enough for Ava's taste. Nolan could sense she was about to cancel their adventure and he quickly interjected.

"Then we're good! We'll be fine, Ava. Don't worry. Now, come on. We're almost there." He smiled uneasily. Ava shook her head, exhaling, but continued the ascent upstairs.

A few more steps and they finally reached Groppy's secret room. Nolan grabbed the knob and turned, pushing the door open. It creaked and the three eagerly peered inside. It was just as Nolan had left it last night. The dust, strange vials, over-stuffed bookshelves, the table with scattered ingredients, and the cauldron with potion left in it. Still murky and still smelly.

"Wow," Ava and Charlotte both exclaimed. They walked around the room, heads turning right and left to look at every little thing.

"This is like out of a fairy tale," Ava admired as she touched a vial marked "Butterfly Tears." "It's incredible."

"What smells funny?" Charlotte asked, holding her nose.

"That's the potion." Nolan pointed to the cauldron.

The children carefully walked over to the fireplace and peered into the black pot. The liquid inside was purple and silent, but smelly.

"And this is where you wished from?" Ava scrunched her nose.

"Yeppers," Nolan smiled brightly. "The recipe for it is on the table." Ava walked over to the open book and looked over the ingredients listed, along with those lying on the table. She held a finger on the page and closed the book, reading the cover.

"Grimoire."

"Yeah, the book has a funny name," commented Nolan.

"It means 'book of spells,'" Ava explained. "I learned about this last Halloween during reading class. Most witches have a grimoire." Ava opened the book back up to where her finger was. "Hmm. A wishing spell." She turned back to Nolan. "Okay, how does it work?"

"Just say, 'I wish,' and then say whatever it is that you want to wish for."

"That's it?"

Nolan shrugged. "That's it." Ava walked back to the cauldron and looked into the purple goo. What should she wish for? She could literally wish for anything she wanted. She opened her mouth to speak but was interrupted by Merlin.

"Be careful with your choice of words because the cauldron will give you whatever you ask for. It's very . . . literal." He stared intently at the pot and flicked his tail. That uneased Ava a little. It annoyed Nolan.

"Don't be such a party pooper, Merlin. Look, it's fine. Watch." He leaned over the cauldron. "I wish for a plate of chocolate chip cookies." The cauldron rumbled and the girls jumped back. A bright light shot out of the pot, and something started to rise from the liquid. Charlotte shrieked. They all watched in fascination as the goo disappeared. Floating above them was a plate of freshly made chocolate chip cookies. Nolan carefully reached out and grabbed the plate. Without thinking twice, he picked up a cookie and ate it.

"Wait!" Ava shouted. "You don't know where those came from."

"They came from magic," Nolan said matter-of-factly and swallowed. "I'm fine. They're just cookies. See?" He handed one to Ava. She slowly reached with her fingers and took hold of the cookie, bringing it to her face for a closer look. She sniffed it. It smelled like a cookie. Felt like one, too. Cautiously, she brought it to her mouth, taking a tiny bite. Warm chocolate chips melted on her tongue, and the sweetness of the cookie made her drool a bit. She wiped the side of her mouth with the back of her hand.

"WOW. This is one delicious cookie," she said, muffled, while taking another bite.

Nolan threw her an "I told you so" look. "See, nothing to worry about."

Charlotte quickly reached up and grabbed a cookie, cramming it into her mouth. "It's so yummy!" she exclaimed through a mouthful of cookie bits.

"What should we wish for next?" Ava asked.

"Whatever you want." Nolan held his hands out. Ava looked at the large pot and thought.

"Okay, I wish . . . " She glanced back at Nolan, who nodded his head in encouragement. "I wish for . . . a notebook and some colored pencils." The cauldron rumbled, light radiated from inside, and a spiral-bound notebook with a box of colored pencils appeared hovering above the pot. Ava grinned, reached out, and grabbed the supplies, holding on tight. This was unbelievable.

Nolan groaned. "Lame. You could have wished for *anything*, Ava, and you wished for school supplies. Use your imagination."

Ava protested. "You said *anything*, and this is what I wanted. All *you've* wished for is food." Ava admired her wish in her hands.

"Whatever," Nolan muttered.

"Well, we know it works. We should be careful, though. It looks like we use a little of the potion every time we make a wish," Ava pointed out as she glanced inside the cauldron, noting that the goo level had gone down. "Wouldn't want Groppy finding out that we came up here."

"The spell book is right there on the table." Nolan jerked his head to the open grimoire. "We can just make more potion."

"Actually," interrupted Merlin, "you would have to be a witch to do that."

"Maybe only small wishes use small amounts of the potion," pondered Ava. "Just wish for small things." She turned to Charlotte. "Okay, Charlotte, it's your turn. Wish for anything you want, but make sure it's small."

"Okay." Charlotte grinned mischievously. She tip-toed over to the pot and closed her eyes, thinking.

"I bet she wishes for another talking cat," Nolan whispered to Ava. They waited and watched their little sister.

"Maybe she doesn't know what to wish for," Ava whispered back. Charlotte's eyes were squeezed shut as she thought hard about her wish. "Charlotte, it's okay if you don't know what you want. You can take your time," Ava said reassuringly.

Charlotte looked at her siblings, a sparkle in her eye. "Oh, I know what I want." She could not contain her excitement. "I wish for a rainbow that tastes like jelly beans."

Nolan made a weird face. "I wasn't expecting that."

Ava twisted her mouth. "I think that's what she dreamed about last night. I heard her talking to Merlin about it this morning." The cauldron rumbled, but before the wish came true, Charlotte opened her mouth to wish *again*.

"Uh, was that *all* she dreamed about?" Nolan asked anxiously. Ava thought quickly. Something in Charlotte's dream had *pooped* jelly beans. *What was it? Come on. Think. Think. Oh, no.*

"Charlotte, don't!"

"I WISH FOR A PONY!"

10

A BRILLIANT AND COLORFUL RAINBOW SHOT OUT OF THE CAULDRON. Everyone scattered. Nolan dodged just in time as the colored light flew straight for his head. Merlin hissed and hid behind a wooden chair in the corner. Ava grabbed Charlotte and pulled her away from the black pot that rumbled so loudly, she thought it might explode.

"I said to wish for something small!" Ava shouted at Charlotte over the thundering sounds of the cauldron. "A pony is *not* small!"

"It's smaller than a unicorn! That's what I *really* wanted!" Charlotte answered back innocently.

Good grief, Ava thought.

Nolan cautiously stuck his tongue out and licked the rainbow. His eyes lit up in surprise. "It tastes just like jelly beans!" he exclaimed enthusiastically to his sisters.

"Now is *not* the time, Nolan!" Ava yelled back, irritated.

"When will we ever get *another* time to lick a rainbow?!" Nolan shot back defiantly.

Ava was going to argue that point when she heard a whinny come from within the cauldron. She turned her head toward the fireplace in time to see a real-life pony leap out of the booming pot. The cauldron finally quieted, leaving a chestnut pony dappled in white spots. The miniature horse neighed and swished its amber mane.

"My pony!" Charlotte shrieked with excitement. She wriggled out of Ava's grasp and ran toward it, waving her arms excitedly.

"Charlotte, don't run! You might scare it!" Ava cautioned. But it was too late. Charlotte had already spooked the timid horse. The spotted pony reared up on its hind legs and whinnied, its tail swishing left and right. Charlotte froze, frightened just a few feet away. Nolan was anxious, but while he kept his eyes on his little sister, his tongue continued to lick the candy rainbow.

The pony reared and swished its tail, knocking over some of the glass vials on Groppy's shelves. They shattered to pieces as they hit the hard-wood floor. One that contained lizard tails broke closest to the horse, sending out squirmy-looking worms that wiggled and writhed. The lizard tails startled the pony, which clopped its hooves, striking the ground. Then it broke into a gallop. Ava quickly climbed onto the table, pulling Charlotte up beside her before the horse knocked her down. Nolan, finally sensing danger, abandoned the rainbow and joined them. The horse ran and bucked wildly around the room.

"What are we going to do?" Ava asked, terrified. The skittish pony continued to gallop, knocking over cases and bookshelves full of fragile containers and old texts. Glass shattered and books flew as it kicked and neighed. The horse stomped on the books, tearing the spines and spreading papers all over the wooden floor. "We have got to get it out of here!" Ava turned toward Nolan, looking for some ideas. Nolan scrunched his forehead and tried to think of something, but nothing came. Merlin jumped from his hiding spot in the corner onto the table, hissing and meowing.

"You might want to do something fast before the pony destroys everything," Merlin pointed out.

"Really?" Ava shouted at the cat.

Charlotte's body was shaking. "Maybe we can wish for another pony. That way it would have a friend and it wouldn't be so scared," she suggested.

"Two ponies would not help the situation, but thank you for trying," Ava replied, trying to sound appreciative.

"But maybe *wishing* something else would work," Nolan said. "I've got it. I wish the pony would disappear!"

The racing pony vanished from sight, but the sound of its crashing hooves stayed. "Be careful with your *choice* of words," Merlin hissed nodding toward the pot. "I told you. It takes things very literally."

"Cheese and crackers, Nolan!" Ava shouted. "You didn't wish it away. You just made it invisible!"

"Ha!" Nolan half-laughed in fear. "I really didn't think this could get any worse." The ancient bookshelf was knocked over and a few of the old, heavy tomes came flying at the kids, who screamed and ducked. Amid the madness, a few lit candles on the table and shelves fell over and caught fire on the fallen books and papers scattered across the floor. It spread across the ancient and yellowed pages with a fierce velocity.

"Fire!" Charlotte pointed. The flames quickly spread from the dried-out pages of the ancient books and climbed rapidly toward the wooden table. The kids yelled and bunched closer together.

"This is bad." Nolan looked at Ava. "I don't know what to do." For once, Nolan would have appreciated Ava's thoughts and advice. Ava thought ferociously of how she could get them out of this, but there was just too much going on.

"There's too much noise!" She grabbed her head. "I can't think!" *I just need a second to think.* Then a thought occurred to her. "I wish the pony was visible and everything, except me, would stop!" The pony was climbing on the table closer to the children, hooves thrashing. The cauldron rumbled. Ava closed her eyes. "Please work," she whispered as chaos filled her ears. The bright light boomed from the fireplace and then . . .

Silence.

Ava slowly opened her eyes and peered out. Nothing was moving. Everything had stopped. She blinked in astonishment. The horse was frozen a foot from Charlotte, hooves reaching toward her, its mane flared out, spiky and full in the air. The fire flames shimmered above books on the floor and table legs, bright red and yellow with blue centers, but they didn't move or grow. Charlotte was holding on tightly to Merlin, who was also holding on tightly to her, his claws dug deep into her pajamas. Ava turned toward Nolan and let out a short laugh. Somehow, she had missed him taking off his shirt and beating the flames near the table. Now that everything was still, she could think.

The best way to clear this all up would be with a wish, but she didn't know how much of the potion was left and she didn't dare move. Hopefully, enough for one more wish. Her words needed to be perfect.

"I can't wish for everything to go back to normal," she thought out loud, "because this place was never *normal* to begin with. So normal would not be right. And if I wish for everything to go away, then I might wish us *all* away, and we could disappear . . . forever." That thought gave her the willies and she shuddered. "But . . . " she continued, "I could wish for everything to return to where it was right before Charlotte's wish." Ava nodded her head. "That might work." She took a deep breath and let it out slowly. "I wish for everything to go back to where it was . . . right before Charlotte's wish." The cauldron rumbled. Ava held her hands and squeezed them anxiously. It was like someone hit the rewind button and time-reversed itself.

The horse galloped backward around the room and went hind legs first, back into the cauldron. The flames receded and flickered to the overturned candles that then turned right-side up. A swirling wind of loose papers danced around Ava as they reconstructed back into books and flew to the bookshelves that were now upright. The shattered pieces of glass reformed into vials, and the spilled liquids and tails slithered back inside. The containers floated back to their right spots on the shelves. Everything was going back to where it was before.

Then, Ava felt a tug as she and her siblings were gently pulled by the magic back to the exact spots they were standing in right before Charlotte made her wish. It worked. The spell had actually worked! Once everything was back to where it was supposed to be, time unfroze. Nolan and Charlotte came out of their trance yelling, then blinked and stared at the room.

"What just happened?" asked Nolan.

"Where did the pony go?" Charlotte wanted to know.

"So, you still remember everything?" Ava asked. The reversal wish hadn't affected their memory.

"It just happened. Of course, we remember," Nolan replied, slightly annoyed. "What did you do?"

Ava explained her wish and her careful choice of words to her brother and sister.

"This is all just nuts," said Nolan. "But good thinking on your part. Nice work, Ava." He gave her a thumbs-up. Charlotte did as well.

"I think we've done enough wishing for one day," said Ava, quite exhausted. For once her brother also nodded in agreement. "I don't even know how long we've been up here. Groppy could come back home any minute." She looked around the walls, but there was no clock. "Ugh. I wish I had a watch." Ava quickly slapped her hands over her mouth, but it was too late. Out from the cauldron popped a silver watch with a rainbow band.

"Whoops." Ava shrugged, embarrassed, and reached out and grabbed it.

Charlotte awed at the colorful watch band. "That's the most beautiful watch I have ever seen."

Nolan walked over to the cauldron and looked inside. "That was the last of it. The potion is all gone."

"Great," Ava said, frowning. "Now Groppy will know we came up here." She glanced at her new watch. "And it's after lunch. We need to go back." Charlotte and Merlin carefully climbed off the table and headed for the door. Ava looked around for her first wish, the notebook and pencils, and found them lying on the table next to the plate of cookies Nolan had wished for. Her mouth turned up into a smile. "At least we have something to eat that's not made of spider legs or lizard tails." She picked up hers and Nolan's wish and headed toward the door.

"I'll be right there!" Nolan said over his shoulder. He spotted a few empty vials on one of the shelves and softly picked them up. Charlotte, Merlin, and Ava were already on the steps outside. Secretly, Nolan went back over to the cauldron, dipped the vials inside, and carefully got the last bit of potion into the two small containers, leaving only a small drop behind. He silently slid them into his pajama pocket. "You never know when you'll need a little magic." He smirked.

"Are you coming, Nolan?" Ava yelled from the steps.

"Yep!" Nolan answered. He ran to his sisters and carefully closed the door behind him.

11

AVA WAS FINALLY ABLE TO BREATHE A SIGH OF RELIEF AS THEY WALKED through the red door and returned to Nolan's room. She was worried that one of Groppy's thousands of cats might have opened the door while they were in the spell room, causing the four of them to be trapped in the stairwell forever.

"So now what?" Nolan asked, already bored. He slumped onto his bed.

Ava scoffed. "Well, I don't know about you, but I've had enough excitement for one day. Let's just relax and wait till Groppy gets back."

"Relax?" Nolan questioned. "Have you forgotten we're staying in a haunted house? How can we relax? Who knows what else she's hiding in this place?"

"That's what I'm afraid of," Ava replied.

"Come on," Nolan nudged. "It's at least daylight. The house isn't as scary when the sun's out."

Ava contemplated this. "Maybe we can explore some. I do wonder why we can't leave the house and why she left so quickly today before breakfast."

"Exploring sounds like fun," Charlotte replied with a purring Merlin in her lap. "I want to explore."

"Then it's settled." Ava nodded. "We'll check out the rest of Groppy's house. But no more hidden stairs."

* * *

After the siblings changed out of their pajamas, they headed downstairs to investigate the rest of Groppy's magical home. Ava called out Groppy's name a few times to see if their great-aunt had returned, but there was no answer. They were home alone.

As they explored, they were greeted by Groppy's army of cats. But now that the cats had gotten used to the children's scents, they didn't attack them like they had the night before. Instead, they just rubbed all over them, nibbling at their pants legs and licking their ankles with their sandpaper tongues.

"Get off!" Nolan shouted at a few furry cats that scurried around his feet, making it impossible to walk. Charlotte couldn't take a step without a cat lying in front of her shoes. Ava had three cats latched onto her pants legs that she dragged with every step.

"Have mercy!" Ava yelled in frustration. "Merlin! Can you not help us here?"

Merlin was walking on the balcony handrail safely away from all the cats. He sighed. "What do you want me to do?"

"Tell them to get their furry butts out of here!" Nolan snapped. Merlin glared at him and then at the cats.

"Get out of here. Go away, cats. Shoo," he said with little to no emotion as he flicked his paw at the mountains of cats.

Ava gawked at him. "I could have done that. Tell them in 'cat' to go away! Meow at them or something."

Merlin licked his paw. "Oh, I don't speak *cat*."

"You have got to be kidding me," Nolan said through clenched teeth as he pulled a cat off his pants leg. He winced as one of the cat's sharp claws pricked his skin.

"But I do know of a trick." Merlin smiled. "Follow me."

Merlin led the kids down the stairs and back into the kitchen to the fridge. Somehow, the children managed to follow as they crawled their way there through the sea of cats. Merlin was waiting for them on the kitchen table.

"These cats LOVE cheese," said Merlin. "Always keep some cheese in your pockets and throw it down whenever you are about to be attacked. They will go for the cheese and leave you alone."

Ava looked skeptical. "Really?"

"Really," Merlin purred.

Nolan opened the fridge and found a block of blue cheese sitting open on a saucer. It smelled awful. He quickly glanced around the rest of the shelves and drawers curiously. There were a lot of vegetables, some unidentifiable meat, and something that looked like mud. He grimaced and pulled out the stinky cheese, broke it into three pieces, and handed it to his sisters, who wrinkled their noses in return.

"This smells like feet," Ava choked.

"Try it out," Merlin said. Ava held her breath and pinched off a small piece of smelly cheese. She waved it around her so the cats clinging to her clothes could smell it, then threw it a few feet away on the ground. Like magic, all the cats meowed and jumped from the kids to the pungent cheese.

"Huh. It worked." Ava raised her eyebrows, astonished.

"Well, of course, it did," Merlin huffed.

Now that the kids could get away from the cats, they ventured down the same hallway they had the night before. As they walked, they threw out pieces of cheese from their pockets, and the cats scattered to run and eat the stinky, moldy dairy. The floors creaked as they made their way to the doors they hadn't explored yet.

Ava first approached the door on the left, turned the knob, and peeked inside. The first thing she saw was a large old wood frame bed covered in cats. A few cats glared up at her and she quickly closed the door. "Yikes, that must be Groppy's room. We're not going in there." She turned her head. "Let's try this one," Ava said, pointing to the one on the right. The door was a little stuck, but with the help of her siblings, they pushed it open. It swung wide to a room lit by one very large window that highlighted all the dust. The room smelled musty, and the kids covered their mouths and noses with their shirts and walked inside.

"It's a library," Ava realized. All the walls were lined with shelves full of books that looked similar to the ones in the spell room. Charlotte pulled one of the books off a lower shelf and flipped through it.

"Where are the pictures?" She sighed, upset.

"Here's one." Nolan grinned, holding up a book with an image of a vampire bat sucking blood from someone's neck. Charlotte shrieked and ran toward Ava while Nolan snickered.

"I don't think these are books like the ones in your school library," Ava said as she patted Charlotte.

A large desk stood below the window. A few books were scattered on top. Ava read through the titles: *Magical Creatures, Myths and Legends of Mystical Folklore, How to Train a Dog, Wolf Ancestry, Wild Canines.* There seemed to be a theme to the books Groppy studied. As Ava flipped through the pages, she noticed Groppy had flagged a few and written notes in the margins. They all said the same thing: *Tried and Failed.*

One old book lay open on the desk. Ava read its title: *The Secrets of Werewolves.* "Why is she looking at books on wild magical animals, and mostly, wild dogs?" Ava thought out loud.

"Maybe she's tired of all her dumb cats," Nolan answered. "I know I am."

Ava waved him off. "Remember the coyotes we heard when we got here? The ones in the woods?" Ava asked. Charlotte nodded. "Groppy told us not to go into the woods this morning, and last night she told us not to go outside because it wasn't safe." Thoughts started forming in Ava's mind as she pieced the clues together. She turned toward her siblings. "What animals like to come out at night to howl at the moon?" Ava asked. Charlotte shook her head. Nolan shrugged. "Wolves," Ava answered. "And what type of mythical wolf comes out when there's a full moon?"

Ava picked up an open book from the desk and showed her siblings the front. The light flickered off the old gray cover. An image was outlined in shiny silver to resemble a large hairy creature standing on two legs, with menacing fangs, long claws, and pointed ears. "Those may have been coyotes that we heard yesterday, but they weren't the only animal howling last night." Nolan blinked and shook his head with realization as he looked from the book cover to Ava.

"You mean," Nolan said, pointing to the book. "Groppy has . . . "

"A werewolf," Ava finished. "And for some reason, she can't get rid of it."

The front door slammed shut and a screeching voice boomed throughout the house.

"Chiiilldreeenn! I'm baaack!"

Ava swiftly put the book back on the desk and, hands flying, rearranged everything to where it had been.

"Quick!" she said to her siblings. "Find something to look at that's *not* about werewolves, and try to act natural." Charlotte and Nolan stood frozen. Ava waved her arms. "That's not natural!"

"I'm scared," Charlotte squeaked. "Is she going to get mad at us?"

"Relax. She told us to stay *in* the house," Nolan replied, a little anxious. "And this is a room *in* the house. We should be fine."

Ava walked over to the bookshelf and found two books as far away from the topic of wolves as possible. She handed one titled *The Magic of Insects* to Charlotte, and the other titled *What's That Smell: Potions Gone Bad* to Nolan. Nolan glanced at the title. "She's obviously not read this one," he muttered.

"Chiilldreeen. Where are yoouuuu?" The stomping of footsteps came down the hall along with a thousand meowing cats.

"Sounds like she forgot to keep cheese in her pocket," Charlotte informed the others.

"Sit on the floor and pretend to read," Ava hissed to both of them. There was only one chair in the room behind the desk, and no one was going to sit there or else Groppy would know they were snooping through her stuff. Charlotte and Nolan promptly sat and flipped through the pages of their books. Ava grabbed one for herself about edible forest plants and sat quickly on the floor right as Groppy approached the door.

"Ahh! So, there you are." She gave a crooked smile as she stepped inside the library. Nolan sneezed from behind the pages of his book. Groppy smelled extra spicy today. "I see you found the library. There are many books here on interesting topics you won't find in a typical library. I have . . . special interests."

"They look like normal books to me," Nolan said, keeping his voice calm. "Right, Ava? Nothing magical about these books." Ava glared at Nolan in a way that said, "Stop talking." He got the hint.

Groppy glanced over at the pile of books on the desk. Her eyes squinted and she tapped at one of the large moles on her face. Ava's mouth twisted as Groppy found a hair in the mole and tugged at it. Nolan made a noise between a gag and cough.

"I'm sorry I was gone most of the day. Why don't you children go to the kitchen? I've brought home some supper." The kids all eyed each other as they slowly got up and placed their books back on the shelf and then left the room. They didn't speak as they stepped out into the hallway. "I'll be there in a minute!" Groppy screeched and the library door slammed behind them.

"That was weird," Nolan whispered, and the siblings walked cautiously to the kitchen to whatever food awaited them.

* * *

The Alexander children sat anxiously around the dinner table waiting for Groppy to come in with dinner. They had expected an awful smell as they entered the kitchen, but it smelled the same as it had that morning, minus the porridge. The cats *had* eaten that. Merlin wasn't joking.

"So . . . what do you think we'll be eating tonight?" Nolan asked, fiddling with a splinter of wood he had pulled off the table. "I don't see anything here."

"Maybe it's in the fridge," Ava said. "What did you see in there when you looked for the cheese?" she asked.

Nolan frowned and shook his head. "You don't want to know."

"Great." Ava scowled, and her stomach growled. Groppy came thudding down the hallway and the kids' backs straightened.

"Well, are you all hungry?" Groppy asked as she walked into the kitchen. "Looks to me like you don't have enough meat on your bones. I need to fatten you up." She cackled and smiled a wicked grin. The kids shuddered, and each gave an uneasy smile in return. "I was going to bake one of my favorite recipes for you, but something came up and I didn't have the time." Nolan, who had been holding his breath, blew it out in relief. "So instead, I picked you up a pizza." Seemingly out of thin air, Groppy produced a pizza box and placed it on the table. The kids looked at it in shock.

"Well." Groppy stared at the children. "Aren't you going to eat?"

Nolan's hand moved toward the box, then hesitated mid-air. "Um, what's on the pizza?" he asked carefully.

"My favorite toppings," Groppy answered.

Nolan squinted. "And would those be considered normal toppings?" Ava kicked his leg from under the table and he winced.

"I *only* eat cheese pizza," Charlotte started to explain, but Ava shot her a look.

"You can *pick* the toppings off, then," Ava muttered back to her little sister. Ava had no idea what was on the pizza, but since she now knew for a fact that Groppy was a witch, she was not going to get on her bad side by appearing ungrateful.

Ava grabbed the box, while her brother and sister watched in anticipation. She closed her eyes and slowly lifted the lid, then peered inside. It was a baked, round dough circle, with cheese and tomato sauce. "Oh, it's a pizza," Ava said, relieved and somewhat disappointed, though she wasn't sure why.

"What were you expecting?" Groppy asked. She twitched her nose, making one of the larger moles on her face wiggle. Nolan leaned over in his chair to get a better look at the pizza.

"Wait a minute." He pointed at the open box, "What's that?"

"It's ham and pineapple," said Groppy. Charlotte stuck out her tongue.

"It looks . . . great," said Ava, glaring at both her siblings. "Thank you, Gropp—I mean Aunt Poppy." She added a quick smile and looked at her brother and sister to do the same.

"Thank you, Aunt Poppy," they both said in unison with less enthusiasm. Groppy was pleased and turned to the fridge.

"*Who* in their right mind puts fruit on a pizza?" Nolan silently muttered to himself while picking the pineapple bits off his slice. "It's as gross as people putting fruit in ice cream. If I wanted to eat something healthy, I would eat fruit by itself, but when I want ice cream, I *want* ice cream. Don't put fruit *in* my ice cream."

"This is yucky." Charlotte turned up her nose. "I'm not eating this." Ava sighed and picked all the ham and pineapple off one slice of pizza and handed it to Charlotte, who eyed it. Finally, she gave in and took a bite. She was really hungry, after all.

"At least it doesn't have spiders or bugs on it," Ava whispered.

"Or worms and lizard tails," Nolan added, chomping into his piece that still had ham on it. He liked ham.

HOOOWWWLLLLLLL.

The kids stared out the window with cheeks full of pizza. Something howled outside in the woods surrounding the house. Groppy closed the fridge door and looked, too. She frowned.

"You children eat up," their aunt said as she headed toward the front door, grabbing a slice of pizza as she did.

"Where are you going?" Charlotte asked.

"Don't worry. I'll be back really quick." Groppy stepped one foot outside, then turned back and eyed the children with her mismatched eyes and said in a serious tone, "Stay inside." She turned away, her long black braid whipping in the air and headed down the steps. The door magically closed behind her with all the bolts locking into place.

12

"She can't just keep leaving the house and *not* tell us where she's going or what's going on," Ava spouted as she sat on her bed. After the kids had finished the pizza, they waited at the table for Groppy but she never came back. As creepy as their great-aunt was, Ava was starting to worry about her. Which was weird.

"She doesn't know that we *know* she's a witch," said Nolan as he lay face down on the black shag rug. He had found that with all the cat hair it had collected, it was surprisingly soft. "She won't tell us anything."

"Well, she should inform us of what's going on," Ava replied while crossing her arms. "I mean, we're as close to the woods as she is, and unlike her, we don't have magical powers. I wouldn't even know what to do if I saw a werewolf."

"Run," came Nolan's muffled answer through the shag rug. Ava rolled her eyes and mouthed back, "Obviously."

Charlotte was sitting on her bed, stroking Merlin's belly, only half-listening. She was more of a cat person, anyway. She didn't much care for dogs . . . or werewolves.

"That's it." Ava hammered her fist into her palm. "Tomorrow I'm going back to the library and reading up on werewolves. I will at least be prepared if one gets in the house. Groppy *can* keep me from going outside, but she *can't* keep me from reading."

"She can keep me from reading." Nolan smiled. Nolan only cared to read comic books. So, unless there was a werewolf comic downstairs, he wasn't interested. Ava looked at her rainbow watch. It was almost ten p.m.

"It's getting late. We need to go to sleep. Got a lot of researching to do tomorrow." Ava walked over to blow out the candles on the walls while Nolan pulled himself off the ground and crawled to his room. "And leave your door open!" she shouted to Nolan. "I can't sleep knowing you're sneaking off to the spell room." Nolan groaned and pushed the red door wide open. She heard him mutter something that sounded like "bossy pants" and "party pooper."

Once Ava tucked herself in, she looked around the moonlit room. Both her siblings were asleep, and Merlin was purring peacefully at the foot of Charlotte's bed. Ava laid her head on her pillow and her mind raced. Tomorrow would be day three at Groppy's. Only a few more nights of sleep till Christmas. They had survived this far. It was easy to forget about presents and holidays when they were staying at a witch's house. Especially when they were stuck inside because of the werewolf that was possibly roaming the woods near them. Ava shifted to her side and listened to the noises outside her window.

"This is insane," she exhaled. "But I need to be prepared for the worst. We have got to make it through till Mom and Dad come back." After a few restless minutes, the chorus of crickets and toads finally lulled her to sleep.

* * *

The next morning began a lot like the previous. Ava woke her siblings up and dragged them downstairs to whatever breakfast Groppy had made for them. Once again, there was another note left for the children. This one was written with a quick and shaky hand. Groppy must have been in a hurry. Their aunt mentioned needing to get some supplies but that she would be back by lunch. On the table was their breakfast—Pumpkin Turnover Surprise.

"They look like normal turnovers," mused Ava.

"But what's the *surprise?*" Nolan rubbed his chin. "Let's make the cat eat one."

"Ha!" Merlin laughed. But just in case, the cat jumped onto the top of the cabinets where the kids couldn't reach.

"It smells like a pumpkin." Charlotte sniffed. She pressed on a turnover with her finger. Her eyes squinted. "There's something in there," she whispered.

"Just open it up," Nolan told her.

Charlotte grimaced but tore the turnover in her hands into two pieces. A black spider fell out and hit the table with a thud. Charlotte screamed and the two pieces of turnover went flying off in different directions. Ava and Nolan also jumped back.

"First fruit on pizza, now spiders in turnovers. Groppy is ruining good food!" Nolan facepalmed and shook his head.

"The spider isn't moving," Ava pointed out. She took a few timid steps closer to the table to examine the eight-legged creature. "Wait a minute . . . " She picked up a fork and poked the spider, then stepped back. It didn't move. "This spider isn't real . . . it's chocolate."

"A chocolate spider?" Charlotte asked.

Ava picked it up and bravely bit off the head. It was delicious milk chocolate, but the shape of the spider was creepily lifelike. "Yeah, that's chocolate, all right."

Nolan waved his hands in the air. "Surprise," he said, unamused. Ava looked at the half-eaten chocolate spider in her hand and nearly choked. The arachnid looked identical to the one that had dangled in front of her when they first arrived at Groppy's.

"Do you think she turned that spider into chocolate?" Nolan asked, his mouth twisted giving a sour look.

"I don't want to think about it," Ava said, then forced herself to swallow the melted chocolate spider.

The kids picked around the turnovers. Then Ava headed to the library with her notebook and pencils, while the other two stayed in the living room. They remembered to grab stinky cheese as they left the kitchen, so periodically they would throw pieces of it on the ground to shoo away the hundreds of cats. Nolan and Charlotte were starting to get used to the sea of fur around them.

Ava read shelves in the library, trying to find any book on magical creatures, interactions with them, or books specifically on werewolves. It was helpful that Groppy still had her books laid out on the desk, and Ava flipped through them, too, taking notes on what she found.

Werewolves are humans that have been bitten by a werewolf and cursed. They turn into werewolves either during a full moon or if they can control their power, whenever they want to. This would explain why there had been a werewolf outside Groppy's for the past few days when the moon wasn't full. That meant that this one must be powerful. *Werewolves have sharp fangs and long claws. They stand on two legs and have eyes that are red like the sun. They are carnivores—meat-eaters.*

"Frightening." Ava trembled. She glanced at her watch. It was getting close to lunchtime. "I better check on the other two. Who knows what they're up to?" She closed the book and headed toward the living room. Charlotte and Nolan had their foreheads smashed against the window and were staring outside when Ava arrived.

"What are you doing?" she asked.

"Well, we already stared at each other and then had a staring contest with the creepy owl portraits," Nolan answered.

"And I won!" Charlotte exclaimed happily. "They blinked first." A few days ago, Ava would have wondered if her sister was going crazy, but not anymore. Ava looked at the owl portraits, who, in turn, stared right back at her with dejected looks. She had always felt that those portraits were alive. Guess she was right about that, too.

"Since *you* won't let us go up the secret stairs, there's nothing else to do in this weird old house, and we can't go outside. So, we're just staring out the window. Bored." Nolan sighed. "And there's nothing good to look at. Nothing but trees and dead grass." He *was* right. The grass was brown and yellow, dry, and crinkly. The wind blew a few bare limbs on the gray trees closest to them, and the few leaves they held shook gently. Crows cawed in the distance. "I can't believe Christmas is in four days. It looks like Halloween around here."

Some evergreens in the distance still had their emerald foliage, adding color to the dull scenery, but something was missing. It didn't *feel* like Christmas. And as Ava continued to look outside, it hit her. Snow.

Their normal holiday was blanketed in thick white snow. Snow that covered everything in sight and made it all sparkle and shine in the sun's rays like it was covered in glitter. Heavy snow that hid all the dull colors of the dying season. That's exactly what was missing. Ava let out a heavy breath, longingly.

"I wish we had snow," she said softly, fogging up the cold window. "Thick blankets of it, like back home. Snow so deep, we could jump into it and it would cover us whole. That's what would make this place look a little nicer. Snow."

Nolan's stomach grumbled incredibly loudly. Ava raised an eyebrow and looked at her brother. "Wow, I guess someone is ready for lunch." Then she noticed his stomach was still rumbling, plus the look on Nolan's face, which appeared to be worried, shocked, and afraid. "Nolan, that's not your stomach, is it?"

Nolan grimaced a smile and held his pocket. "No," he whispered. Ava's nostrils flared as a bright light shot out of Nolan's side pants pocket.

"Nolan." She tried to speak calmly. "What did you do?"

"Heads up!" he shouted. Nolan flung the vial of potion out of his pocket. It burst mid-air and the kids covered their heads with pillows from the couch. A large snow cloud appeared from the broken vial, along with strong freezing winds. Thick snowflakes fell to the wooden floor. A blizzard was forming inside the house. All of Groppy's hundreds of cats ran in a panic. They roared, hissed, clawed, and scratched, trying to keep their fur dry from the falling wet flakes.

"You said the cauldron was empty!" Ava shouted at her brother over the cold gusts of wind. "Empty!"

"I'm sorry!" Nolan shouted back. "I thought it might be useful to have some magic just in case of an emergency."

"You should have told us!" Charlotte poked a finger at him. The snow was falling fast, and Ava and Nolan were already covered in frozen flakes up to their knees. Apparently, they had been wrong about bigger spells needing large amounts of potion. The snow swiftly crept up to Charlotte's stomach. Merlin, being light, ran on top of the snowy hills to the kids, flicking his feet as he did. He did *not* like wet paws.

"Quick, get to the stairs!" Merlin ordered. "We'll be safe in the spell room." Nolan and Ava pulled Charlotte out of the snow, and Ava carried her as they pushed further into the blizzard, trying to find the stairs. The frigid air and swirling snowflakes made it difficult to see. Nolan followed the black cat blindly with Ava and Charlotte close behind. The snow was now up to their waists, and soon they wouldn't be able to move at all.

"I can't f-f-feel my legs," Nolan stuttered.

"Just k-k-keep moving, Nolan!" Ava encouraged, but was worried because she couldn't feel her legs, either. Charlotte shuddered in her arms. They weren't dressed for a blizzard. They would get sick if they stayed in the snow too much longer. Nolan took another struggled step and his foot hit something hard.

"We reached the st-stairs!" he exclaimed, somewhat relieved. He grabbed onto the white-covered handrail and pulled his body out of the snowbank. It wasn't easy. The stairs were covered in snow, but not as much as the living room. Nolan turned to help Ava and Charlotte up and out of the snow. They all held on the rail and climbed.

"It's getting worse!" Ava shouted at Nolan. Snow started to pile onto the stairs. "Go faster!" The kids quickly climbed the stairs and reached the top. They started to run down the balcony toward the bedroom door, but a tall snowdrift had formed in front of it.

"Help me get to the door!" said Nolan, digging for the frozen doorknob. Together the siblings tried to dig their way to the door, but it was no use. The snow was too heavy and thick.

"I wish I had grabbed the other potion," Nolan stressed, staring helplessly at the snow now up to his knees.

"Other potion?" Ava held out her hands. "How much potion was left?"

Nolan shrugged. "Just enough for two vials. I'm sorry!"

"Umm," Charlotte said muffled.

"What?" Ava said, irritated, and turned to see her sister covered to her neck in snow. How had it gotten so deep so quickly? "Charlotte!" Ava tried to move to help her little sister but found herself buried to her belly button. Ava couldn't climb out. "Oh no. Oh, no, no, no!" Ava struggled and kicked with her arms and feet, pushing snow away from her, trying to make steps to climb out, but it was no use. She was too cold. She couldn't move. "Charlotte! Cover your mouth with your hands. Make an air pocket so you can breathe!"

Nolan couldn't move either, and he started to freak out. "Merlin!" Nolan shouted. "Help us!" Nolan heard paws running across snow away from them. Merlin was their only hope now.

"How can a cat help . . . ?" Ava started to say, but snowflakes reached her mouth and she had to shut it. Her whole body was trembling. What would happen to her? What would happen to her brother and sister? The wind howled as the snow continued to fall. It was almost to her ears. Nolan started chomping down on the snow. Maybe he could eat his way out. Ava squeezed her eyes tightly. "I wish Groppy was here."

SLAM.

Downstairs, the front door burst open, nearly falling off the hinges. Groppy stepped inside the house, her magic melting a path to the living room, right below where the children were frozen in the snow on the balcony. Ava and Nolan's ears perked up and their bodies stopped shaking.

"Merlin's beard," Groppy muttered as she gazed at the snowy chaos. She cracked her old fingers and held her hands up toward the snow cloud.

"Feran snaw! Feran ceald! That's ENOUGH!!" she bellowed throughout the house. Her voice carried like the winter wind.

Immediately warmth engulfed the crooked house. The sun shone brightly through the open door and windows, and piles of snow started to melt away, flowing like a steady river out the front door. Ava began to regain feeling in her limbs and pushed on the snow pile, bursting out of her now soft and squishy snow cocoon. She rushed for Charlotte and hugged her. They were both dripping wet and shivering.

"I'm, o-okay," Charlotte whispered into her shoulder.

The sun's rays dried all the wood floors, walls, furniture, and even the children's clothes. The siblings looked around, amazed as Groppy's magic cleared out all the frosted white snow and returned the house back to its creepy normal.

"We were almost frozen Popsicles," Nolan said, shaking out a few more bits of snow from his hair. He grinned at Charlotte, who smiled back, but Ava was still upset with Nolan. She shook her head and opened her mouth to give him a piece of her mind when large and heavy footsteps thudded up the stairs, stopping her.

A scratchy and tired voice called out, making the children shiver all over again, and it wasn't because they were just covered in frigid snow.

"Who's been wishing on my cauldron?"

13

No one spoke. Groppy stood in front of the Alexander siblings, hands on her hips, mouth turned in a scowl. A few rogue snowflakes clung to her long dark braid. Ava felt sick to her stomach.

"Is nobody going to tell me?" she asked quietly. Nolan stood silent, biting his fingernails while Charlotte fidgeted and wrung her t-shirt in her hands. Ava put an arm around her sister, noticing she was shivering from fear now instead of cold. Apparently, she would have to be the one to speak up. Ava opened her mouth to explain, but when she looked Groppy in her mismatched eyes, she found it was terrifying and impossible to speak.

Groppy leaned in closer to the kids, causing them to hold their breath. She smelled a bit sweaty today along with the usual spice. "You can't tell me you didn't go up the forbidden stairs." Her voice creaked. "There was a blizzard *in* the house." She leaned back and let out a long, loud cackle. "That doesn't happen every day. Now, *who* wished for it?"

Nolan looked over at Ava, who was now staring down at the floor, gripping her hands tightly. Ava let out a shaky sigh and began to confess but was surprisingly interrupted by her brother.

"It was me," Nolan said. He looked up at Groppy, her mouth still a frown. "I found the stairs and wished on your cauldron. It's my fault about the blizzard, too. I snuck some of the potion in my pocket. I'm . . . sorry." Ava was stunned. Nolan had confessed and taken all the blame. This was more unexpected to her than nearly freezing in a blizzard inside a house.

After his apology, the kids all tensed. They thought Groppy would go berserk, cast spells on them, and maybe turn them into chocolate like she did those spiders and eat them, but she didn't. In fact, Groppy smiled, which undecidedly may have been more disturbing.

"Thank you, Nolan. I know that was difficult. But I don't think it's *all* your fault. Someone would have had to tell you how to find the secret stairs. Or should I say, some *cat*." Groppy spat and fixed her eyes on Merlin, who was attempting to sneak out of the room. She snapped her fingers. The cat flailed as it was lifted in the air and brought to sit in front of the kids. Merlin shrank back and hissed.

"All right, cat. How did you get back in the house? I thought I put you in time-out," Groppy hissed back. Merlin licked his paw casually to appear unfazed.

"Your magic can't keep me out. I'm a clever cat," Merlin purred. Groppy didn't bat an eye.

"No, I think not." She leaned in closer to Merlin, nearly touching his whiskers with her long, pointed nose. "One of these little kiddies let you in, didn't they?"

Merlin flicked his tail. "Maybe. Maybe not. But, even if they did, I wouldn't tell you."

Nolan softly exhaled. Groppy chuckled deep within her throat. "Oh, Merlin. I'll deal with you later." She looked back up at the children, who looked back with uncertain wide eyes. Groppy picked absentmindedly at her braid and flipped it over her back.

"So, you found the spell room and made a wish. I'm impressed you didn't accidentally turn each other into toads." She looked directly at Nolan. "How did you know to make a wish?"

Nolan's eyes flickered briefly to Merlin and then back to Groppy. "You, um, left your spell book open on the table. I read it." He flinched. Groppy rubbed her chin.

"I could erase your memory." The kids startled and looked at Groppy with frightened eyes. "Meh." She waved a warty hand. "Too finicky. Might erase too much."

"You don't need to erase anything," Ava jumped in cautiously. "We kind of guessed already that you were a, uh, umm . . . " She looked at Groppy's shoes and fell silent.

HALLIE CHRISTENSEN

"Mhh hmm," Groppy mused. "Okay, then. Kids, I've decided to leave your memories alone and let you in on my secret, but I think you might already know what it is."

"You like cats?" Charlotte guessed quietly, still wrinkling her shirt.

"You eat spiders?" Nolan also guessed. His nose twitched as he asked.

"Oh," Charlotte interrupted again, "you're backed up. That's why you eat prunes. Nolan told me. It's okay."

Ava looked bewildered at her siblings and huffed. "She's a witch!" Then turning to Groppy, she asked, less confident, "You're a witch, aren't you?" Groppy nodded. "Do my parents know?"

Groppy shook her head. "No, surprisingly. None of the family does. Just you. Everyone else just thinks I like Halloween and the color black," she said while gesturing to her clothes.

"But you wear colorful witch socks, too," Charlotte pointed out.

"Well," Groppy smirked, "they are technically Halloween socks, and I do like the holiday. It's my favorite. You see, most adults don't believe that witches exist. But you kids do. They believe things are just a coincidence, but you knew it was magic."

"So," Ava asked casually, "now that we know that secret . . . can you tell us where you've been going every day and why we can't go outside?" Groppy scratched at a mole on her chin and shrugged.

"Fine. I guess I can't hide that from you now. But let's go downstairs and I'll explain. I need to sit."

* * *

They went to the living room. Groppy sat down in an old wooden chair that creaked loudly under her weight. The siblings gathered around her on the floor. Merlin kept his eye on Groppy and sat closest to Charlotte. He felt safest there.

"So," Ava asked, "how did you become a witch?"

Groppy tilted her head and closed her eyes, thinking. "I don't know that I ever *became* a witch," she replied. "One day I just noticed that if I really focused my mind on something, I could make it happen." She looked over at the couch where a pillow now floated. The kids were astonished as they watched it hover in the air and then fall on top of Merlin. Nolan snorted.

"Was that necessary?" The cat growled and shook his head. Groppy smirked.

"Once I knew I had a special gift, I went searching for books on how to perfect my magic. As you saw in my library, I have quite a collection. Each book made my magic stronger and helped me better understand how to make it work. Most spells require potions, smaller things I can do on my own. Some require words or symbols drawn in the dirt. Some even require the weather." Ava was fascinated.

"And are there other witches or wizards? Or magical creatures?" she asked. "Near here?"

"Yes and no." Groppy nodded her head. "I'm the only witch around here. But, deep in these woods there are magical creatures," she began. "Creatures that you read about in fantasy books and fairy tales. They live within these woods. But . . . " Groppy held up a curved finger. "They cannot get out because I have cast a spell that keeps them safely inside. They live there peacefully, and we don't bother each other, mostly. It's been that way for years."

"So, you're like a protector, like a park ranger?" Ava asked. She had been to many national parks and knew all about the rangers. Groppy thought about it and moved her head from side to side.

"Something like that, yes."

"Is there a dragon in there?" Nolan asked eagerly.

"Maybe my pony went into the woods!" Charlotte realized with excitement.

"Your pony?" Groppy asked, confused.

"Umm, nothing." Ava quickly quieted her sister.

"What about the dragon?" Nolan persisted.

Groppy stared at Nolan but ignored his question. "Anyway," she continued, "I am the protector, and I make sure no magical creature or human gets hurt. But something tore a small hole in my magical shield. I blame the rabbits. They're always nibbling on stuff that doesn't belong to them. Like my herbs and plants."

"But if it's just a small hole, then why not fix it?" Ava remarked.

"That's the thing," Groppy replied. "It's so small, I haven't been able to find it. But someone else did and somehow managed to slip through the magical side and into ours. It's unfortunate, but if there is a breach in the shield, anything can get out once it finds the opening. I need to find a stronger spell for the shield." Her voice trailed off. "I don't think I should be telling you all of this."

"A dragon! I knew it! A dragon found the hole, didn't it?" Nolan jumped up, thrilled.

Groppy frowned, making the moles near her mouth sag. "*If* there was a dragon in the woods, and *if* it did get out, I wouldn't tell you." His joy deflated, and Nolan sat back on the floor muttering something about being in "a house full of party poopers."

"It's not a dragon." Groppy sighed. "It's a werewolf."

"Is that why all the coyotes are howling?" Ava questioned.

"Yes." Groppy nodded. "They are trying to hide from the werewolf. They're frightened. They warn each other with their howls. That's how I know he's . . . near the house. I've been trying to capture him and get him back in the magical realm, but it hasn't been easy. He's too quick and clever. I've tried so many spells to catch him or cause him to go into a deep sleep, but none work. He seems impervious to my magic."

"Im . . . pervious?" Charlotte titled her head, questioning.

"It means her magic doesn't work against the werewolf," Ava quickly explained.

Charlotte nodded, somewhat understanding. "Maybe he likes cheese. The cats like cheese. You could set up a trap with cheese."

Groppy laughed. "Maybe. I'll try that next time."

"And we will help you." Ava nodded. "We want to help, right?" She looked at her siblings.

Nolan agreed first. "Oh, yeah! I want to see a werewolf. That would be awesome."

Groppy shook her head. "That's nice of you, children, but no. You cannot help me with this. It is too dangerous, and you could get severely hurt." She paused and added quite seriously, "Or even killed."

Ava sucked in a breath, but Nolan grew more excited. "I could easily outsmart a werewolf," he said, sure of himself. "It's just a big dog."

"You do know a werewolf is human, too." Ava turned to her brother. "He can turn himself into a werewolf. A seven-foot-tall vicious werewolf with sharp fangs and claws to bite you with."

"Yeah." Nolan looked off to the side. "I knew that."

"Wait," Ava said, "why can't you just catch him when he turns back into a human?"

"I tried," said Groppy. "I never can find him in the daylight. He stays well hidden. And then at night, he's a werewolf."

"Then make a big cloud at night," said Nolan. "Cover the moon."

"The animal in him can still sense the moon when he is outside, whether or not he can see it. Trust me, I have tried. But enough about the werewolf. Back to the secret room. Did you use up all my wishing potion? I had just made a new batch a couple of days ago."

"Well . . . " Nolan scratched his head. "How many wishes can you make with one pot of potion?"

"Thirteen," Groppy answered flatly. "And I had already used some of it before you did."

"Umm." Nolan clenched his teeth. "We may be close."

"How close?" Groppy asked as she leaned toward him.

Nolan counted on his fingers and mumbled, "There was the grilled cheese, cookies, Ava's lame notebook and pencils, Charlotte's rainbow and po . . . uh, stuffed animal pony, Ava's watch, and . . . " He mumbled a few other things and then looked up. "We might be at twelve or thirteen now," he figured, nervously. He specifically didn't mention the other vial of potion back in his room.

"Thirteen wishes and you only nearly ruined the house and froze yourselves once. I'm impressed," Groppy remarked.

"There was a fire, too," Charlotte added, happy to remember something but then quickly silenced herself once she saw the looks of horror on her siblings' faces.

"Merlin's beard," Groppy grumbled. "Okay, well, I'm going to check my spell room to make sure it's *still* there. Since you now know I'm a witch, let's make this simple. What would you like for lunch?"

"A tuna sandwich with Cheetos, BBQ chips, double-fudge brownies with extra thick icing, and a large soda," Nolan blurted out in one breath. Ava gave him a sidelong glance. "What?" he asked. "You want another *surprise* turnover?" He whispered the last part. Ava shrugged. He had a point.

"I would like a BLT with plain chips. Water is fine," Ava said and remembered to add, "Thank you."

"What about you, little one?" Groppy asked Charlotte.

"I want a peanut butter and jelly sandwich with chocolate cake and chocolate milk."

"I think I can handle that," Groppy said with a nod. The kids headed toward the kitchen. Groppy waved her hand over the table, and plates popped up in front of them. With another snap of her fingers, their lunches appeared on their plates, fresh and ready to eat.

"So, how come sometimes you snap your fingers, and sometimes you shout things?" Nolan asked, his mouth full of tuna and chips.

"It depends on how much power the spell will take. Simple ones I can just handle with a snap of my fingers. Larger ones, like house blizzards"—she cut her eyes toward Nolan—"require more powerful verbal commands."

Nolan didn't ask any more after that.

* * *

Ava, Nolan, and Charlotte enjoyed a mostly quiet and uneventful afternoon in Groppy's library, which Ava was grateful for. Nolan and Charlotte played with the cats while Ava researched more on ways to catch a werewolf. Even if Groppy wouldn't let them go outside and help, maybe Ava could find an answer inside reading through books. Groppy went back to the woods and continued to look for the small hole in the magical realm. She didn't return until supper, which was pizza, again, but this time with normal toppings—like cheese and pepperoni. They were halfway through their stay, and the children's original fear of surviving with their great-aunt was starting to wane. Though the house was still spooky and odd, they found it unique and interesting. And Groppy, though still a bit creepy, was, honestly, pretty cool.

As Ava lay in bed that night, she felt almost content and confident that they might actually survive this stay with Groppy. It had been kind of fun so far in a somewhat terrifying way. She turned her head and saw Nolan asleep in his bed and Charlotte asleep in hers with

Merlin curled up at her feet. Tonight, Ava would easily be able to fall asleep, not dreading the next day. Everything was going to be all right. Well, besides the killer werewolf outside the house, everything was all right-ish. Good enough for now. Ava closed her eyes and fell asleep.

But though he looked asleep, Nolan was not. He wanted to see the werewolf and would not take no for an answer. This was a once-in-a-lifetime opportunity. He could take care of himself. He was a big kid, after all. Groppy was just being a typical over-protective adult. Nolan waited patiently for his sisters to fall asleep, then quietly grabbed the second vial of potion hidden under the bed and placed it in his pocket. Tiptoeing softly, he left the bedroom and headed downstairs.

The moon shone brightly through the windows in the living room, which helped him see the hundreds of sleeping black cats. Nolan successfully maneuvered over each slumbering fluffy pile so he didn't wake them up and get scratched to death. Then he silently unlocked all the deadbolts and locks from the front door, slipped outside, and headed for the deep, dark woods.

What he didn't know was that two little eyes had been watching him the whole time. Staying hidden from Nolan's sight, their footsteps softly followed him through the house and into the magical and inky woods.

* * *

Merlin awoke feeling a bit chilly. He blinked his eyes and stared around the children's bedrooms. Nolan's bed was empty. Merlin turned his head back around to his own bed, troubled. Charlotte was missing, too.

14

CRICKETS SKITTERED AND CHIRPED, AND TOADS CROAKED LOUDLY AS Nolan moved further into the dense woods. Each sound of his footsteps made a soft crunch as he stepped on dewy leaves that lay scattered on the forest floor. But all Nolan could hear was the thudding of his heartbeat. *This was a bad idea*, he thought, and wondered if he'd had any good ideas the past few days.

Inside the house, it had been easy to be brave, but he had forgotten how dark the night could be and how scary the woods were without someone there beside you. Nolan kept his hand near his pocket in case he might need a little help from magic. He took a few more steps and then stopped and listened. Something crunched from somewhere behind him. Nolan froze. He waited. Whatever it was, it waited, too.

A large pine tree towered a few feet in front of Nolan, and he swiftly moved behind it to hide. In his mind, he wished his sisters were there with him—or, good grief, even Groppy—but he didn't dare say it out loud or he would waste the potion. Taking a deep breath, he gradually peered out from behind the tree into the darkness. Nothing was there. The clouds that covered the moon shifted, and light shone down into the shadowy woods.

HOOWWWLLLL. HOWLL. HOWLLLLL.

"Coyotes," Nolan breathed shakily. They were not far away. What had Groppy said about the coyotes' call? The high-pitched howls continued. Nolan could hear movement somewhere deeper in the woods. Then he remembered. Groppy said they howled to protect each other. They howled to warn the others that the werewolf was near. Nolan swallowed and his heart beat faster. The coyotes were moving toward him.

* * *

Merlin looked around both bedrooms for Nolan and Charlotte before he jumped on Ava's bed. With his paw, he patted her face. She swiped it away and turned on her side, still sleeping. Merlin sighed, walked up to Ava's hair, and batted it fiercely with his clawed paws. That woke her up. Ava sputtered, hands flying, feet kicking, as she sat up in bed and stared bewildered at Merlin.

"What on earth was that for?" she panted, catching her breath. Merlin only stared.

"I tried to wake you nicely, but it didn't work."

"Well"—Ava smoothed her pajama top and bedsheets—"what did you need in the *middle* of the night?"

"Oh, I don't need anything," Merlin replied. "But I'm sure Charlotte and Nolan do."

"Do what?" Ava questioned, but her eyes jerked from one empty bed to the other, then back to Merlin. "Where are they?"

Merlin flicked his tail. "I have no idea. But if I had to guess, I bet they went to find the werewolf."

Ava's heart nearly stopped.

* * *

Charlotte was getting tired of the big kids going out and having fun on adventures. She was always left out. She was *too small* and *too young*. She would *make a mistake* or *get herself hurt*. It was always *too scary* for a little kid like her. She had watched her brother and sister make plenty of mistakes, get hurt and scared, and yet they still got to go out and have fun.

Charlotte *knew* Nolan would want to find that werewolf, and she knew he would sneak out. He was brave and not afraid of anything. She decided that night to pretend to be asleep and watch for her brother to leave the room. It was hard staying up that late, and she almost fell asleep once, but she forced herself to stay awake. Sure enough, she watched through squinted eyes as Nolan tiptoed silently out of the room and down the stairs. Making sure not to wake Ava or Merlin, Charlotte quietly slid out of her bed and followed.

Nolan was much bigger than Charlotte. He took large steps and moved swiftly. Charlotte saw him go into the woods and she tried to keep up, but it was difficult in the dim light. She soon lost him in the dark and thick forest. Now she was alone. There were sounds and shadows and creepy crawling things everywhere. She tried to call out for Nolan, but all that escaped her throat was a wimpy squeak. She was terrified.

Something darted ahead of her in the woods and Charlotte froze. The moon emerged from behind the clouds. Her eyes squinted to see what it was, but there was nothing there. At least, nothing she could see. Many voices howled in the distance.

HOOWWWLLLL. HOWLL. HOWLLLLL.

"Ack!" Charlotte tried to scream but felt suffocated. Her heartbeat was racing. She looked around for a place to hide and forced her little feet to move forward. She heard more howling and rushed movements in the woods. Charlotte stopped and listened to paws thudding on the forest floor, the snapping of twigs, and the crunching of dead leaves. Whatever it was, it was moving away from her at a lightning speed. Her thoughts worried her. Were they chasing someone or were they running away from something?

* * *

Nolan ran. The coyotes nearly trampled him as he jumped out of the way and into a large bush, which scratched his arms and legs and tore at his pajama shirt. He held his breath as they raced by, completely ignoring him. The coyotes were the size of a dog and very lean, with shaggy gray and tan fur. Their teeth glistened in the moonlight while their tongues hung out the sides of their mouths as they panted from exhaustion.

It seemed like hours, but it was only a few minutes until all the coyotes had passed him. Nolan turned his head and listened for more movement, but there was only silence. When he felt it was safe, he gently maneuvered his body out of the tangled bush and crouched down low.

SNAP.

Something stepped on a stick nearby, and it wasn't Nolan.

SNAP. CRUNCH.

Nolan stilled and moved his head to find where the sound came from. He couldn't see anything. Another cloud had covered the moon, and it was too dark. But something else was still out there.

RUSTLE. RUSTLE.

Nolan jerked around as one of the bushes near him shook. He took a step back and tripped over a tree root. Bright eyes flickered in the brush pile. They were staring straight at Nolan. He reached for the potion in his pocket when something black leaped out and landed on his hand. Nolan yelled and thrashed away, but the animal clung to him. This was too small to be the werewolf, but it still had very sharp claws. Nolan's free hand found a broken branch on the ground. He gripped it tightly and raised it above him, ready to swing at the beast.

"Don't even think about it!" the beast hissed. Nolan knew that voice. His arm halted.

"Ma . . . Merlin?" Nolan whispered. His voice was hoarse and dry.

"Yes, you insane kid, it's me. Here to save you." Merlin padded closer to the frightened boy's face; his whiskers grazed Nolan's chin.

"And me," an irritated, terrified, and unhappy voice sounded behind Merlin. Nolan sank further into the dirt floor. He looked away as Ava's face came into view, lit by a small flickering candle. "You've done some brainless stuff, Nolan, but this takes the cake. Didn't you hear the coyotes howling? You could have died out here!"

"But I didn't. See! I'm still alive." Nolan gestured to himself. "You don't always have to watch out for me, ya know? I've got this." He brushed himself off and stood up. "I don't always need help from my *big* sister." Ava crossed her arms.

Merlin looked around. "Um, Ava," he meowed.

"Oh, *you've* got this?" she huffed. "What were you thinking? Groppy is a witch and she can't find a way to trap the werewolf, but *you* were going to, all by yourself, with no help?"

"Ava," Merlin said again, his ears turning left and right.

"I wasn't going to trap it," Nolan protested. "I just wanted to see it. Also . . . " Nolan reached in his pocket and pulled out the vial of potion. "I was going to escape with magic." He smirked. "In case I needed it." Ava glared at the potion and shook, her hands balled into fists.

Nolan took a step back. He wasn't sure what was worse at the moment—a loose werewolf in the forest or his angry older sister. Ava took one step toward him but stopped. She exhaled heavily and shook her head. Merlin walked around and sniffed the air.

"I don't even know what to say. When will you ever take anything seriously, Nolan? This isn't some video game, and this isn't one of your superhero comics. This is *real*. And I know you think I'm bossy, but I care about you, you insane goofball. Sometimes you have to think of others before you do something crazy." Nolan looked away. Ava shrugged. "Well, come on. We need to get back before the real werewolf finds us." She looked around. "Where's Charlotte?"

"That's what I've been trying to tell you!" Merlin hissed.

Nolan stared at his sister, confused. "Charlotte? What do you mean?"

Ava stepped toward her brother and looked around him. "She followed you out here. She's not with you?"

"I can't smell her," Merlin said, sniffing the air. "But I smell something . . . "

Now, Nolan started to panic.

"No. I haven't seen her at all. She's out here?" Nolan said.

A crash thudded in the woods, followed by a loud, low, growl. Nolan and Ava stiffened as heavy footsteps stomped through the forest.

"I don't think that's a coyote," Nolan whispered. He glanced at Ava's candle. "You need to blow that out. It will see the light and come after us." Ava held the candle away from Nolan's reach and shook her head, looking grim.

"I'd rather him find us than Charlotte."

"Charlotte," Nolan breathed as he looked toward the heavy sounds.

* * *

Charlotte stayed hunkered down by the tree. The howling had stopped a while ago, and she couldn't hear racing paws thundering through the woods. Maybe it was now safe to leave.

She wanted to go back to her bed and cuddle up with Merlin, but when she turned around, she couldn't remember how to get back to Groppy's. She had lost which way she was going, and in the dark, everything looked the same. Charlotte felt tears sting her eyes and abruptly wiped them away. She sucked in a breath and turned to the path that she thought led back to Groppy's house and started walking.

The air was chilly, and Charlotte hugged herself as she continued on the dark path. Occasionally, the moon would pause playing hide-and-seek with the clouds and give her a little light. She couldn't tell if she was going in the right direction, but she kept moving. The moon peeked out again and Charlotte thought she saw a clearing in the woods up ahead. Feeling relieved, she walked faster. Then she stopped. There were footsteps other than her own in the woods. Charlotte took a few more steps. Her steps made a soft crunch, but the other footsteps made a loud *STOMP*.

"Nolan? Is that you?" Charlotte whispered. A snarl answered. Charlotte froze and slowly turned her head toward the snarling sound. Again, the moon moved from behind the clouds, and she could see a dark, large shadow standing by one of the trees not far from her. The shadow's head turned to face her and stared with two glowing red eyes. Suddenly, Charlotte found her voice and let out a loud, piercing scream.

Not far away, Nolan and Ava jumped. The scream was very close. They both looked at each other and began racing toward the sound. Merlin padded a few steps ahead of them. It was difficult dodging bushes, fallen limbs, and trees. A few branches scratched at Ava's face, but she kept on running. Her candle's flame extinguished as she continued in the dark.

Back in the clearing, the werewolf stepped out from behind the shadows and lumbered toward Charlotte. She couldn't move. The animal was tall, like a tree, with dark gray and black fur. Its head was large with a huge mouthful of sharp fangs that were bared and dripping with saliva. It had long arms and legs like a man, but instead of hands and feet, there were paws and claws. But what scared her the most were those glowing red eyes. All she could do was watch as it came closer to her, grinning.

CRASH.

Nolan, Ava, and Merlin thundered into the thicket, briefly startling the werewolf. Ava ran to Charlotte and hugged her. Nolan stood in front of them and waved his arms.

"Stay away from my sisters!" he shouted bravely. Light fell over the werewolf and Nolan's eyes widened in horror. The wolf's tongue lashed out as it sniffed the air. What had he been thinking coming out here alone? Ava looked up at the werewolf and choked on a scream. Nolan stumbled back to his sisters as the beast advanced. It reached out its large paws, catching Nolan's shirt, but he ripped free. Merlin jumped on the werewolf's back, digging his claws into the wolf's flesh. The werewolf let out a howl.

Hurriedly, Nolan grabbed hold of both of his sisters. "I wish we were back inside Groppy's house!" Then quickly he added, "Everyone here BUT the werewolf!"

The werewolf swatted with its huge paw and slung Merlin to the ground with a thud. Charlotte cried out and reached for him. The potion rumbled and lit up the night sky, causing the large beast to stagger back.

The Alexander children felt their bodies tingle as everything grew dark. The kids shut their eyes and held on to each other tightly. A few moments later, the sounds of the wood vanished, and all was quiet. Ava blinked her eyes open. They were all three back in their bedroom. They were safe. The werewolf was nowhere in sight.

Ava felt something warm and wet on her arm and glanced down. She saw it was tears and looked to her sister, concerned. Charlotte was crying. "Charlotte, it's okay. We're fine now and safe inside Groppy's house." Ava wiped her sister's tears away.

"Why am I always so scared? I saw the werewolf and I couldn't even move my feet." Charlotte sobbed.

"It's okay, Charlotte," Nolan said, putting a hand on his little sister's shoulder. "We were scared, too." Ava and Nolan held on to Charlotte a little while longer. They stayed this way until they noticed something small and black lying motionless on Charlotte's bed.

15

As soon as they had found Merlin injured on Charlotte's bed, they knew they had to get Groppy. Though still unnerving, the kids walked down the darkened stairway and hall to their aunt's bedroom on the first floor. Charlotte gingerly cradled Merlin in her arms. A few tears slid down her puffy red cheeks. The children found Groppy's door unlocked. Quickly, they stepped inside the dark room and tiptoed to Groppy, who was snoring loudly in her bed.

It took a lot of little pokes by Ava and shoves by Nolan until Groppy finally snorted awake. She was shocked to see the kids in her room, but her mismatched eyes immediately noticed the fluffy black kitty in Charlotte's arms, and she frowned. Without saying a word, Groppy got up and shuffled toward the door.

The kids noticed that her door was also red with an old golden doorknob, just like theirs. The witch changed the knob from left to right and opened the door, revealing the staircase. Then Groppy, Ava, Nolan, and Charlotte, who was holding Merlin, headed up the candlelit steps of the secret stairwell. As they climbed the stairs, they told Groppy what had happened in the woods.

Once inside the spell room, Groppy pulled out a few dusty books from her bookcase and flipped through the pages. She found one that she liked and began grabbing ingredients off the shelves and mixing them in her cauldron. Ava and Nolan offered to help' and Groppy obliged. They were anxious and worked quickly. As she called out different items on the list, they both read the shelves until they found the correct vials and handed them to her: eye of

6newt, unicorn hair, witch hazel, spotted owl feather, beetle's leg, pig's blood, and lavender.

Some of the ingredients had to be ground down into a fine powder. Groppy placed the ingredients in a bowl and used a rock to crush and stir. Finally, the potion was complete and she poured it into the cauldron and stirred while the fire blazed. She ladled a tiny amount of the liquid out, and Charlotte helped to hold Merlin's small mouth open as Groppy poured the red potion in. Ava and Nolan waited quietly and somberly for them to finish.

"Did it work?" Charlotte asked hopefully after they placed the last drop in Merlin's mouth.

"We won't know until much later today. He was hurt pretty badly." Groppy sighed. She saw the sadness on Charlotte's face and quickly added, "But he's a stubborn cat, and strong, too. He should be all right." Groppy softly placed Merlin on an old blanket in the room. The kids each gave the cat a light stroke on the head and left. When they reached the red door and walked through it, they found themselves back in Groppy's room. Nolan looked around, a bit confused.

"So, how exactly do these doors work?" he asked Groppy.

"All the red doors are magical and lead to the staircase and my spell room. Obviously, you know how to switch the doorknob."

"So, we could get there from our bedroom door, too?" asked Ava.

"Yes." Groppy nodded. "And once you come back, the doorknob switches back to the nonmagical side. But," she said with a slightly stern tone, "you have all had *enough* exploring for tonight." She glanced at the grandfather clock on her wall. "And now it's tomorrow. You need to go to bed. I would lecture you, but I believe you have learned it's best to not go out in the woods at night . . . alone." She stared at Nolan. He looked away. "You could have easily gotten yourselves killed." Groppy pointed a crooked finger at each kid. "Each of you promise me you won't ever go back into those woods, again . . . unless I'm there with you."

Nolan looked up, shocked. "You mean, you'll let us go with you when you hunt down the wolf?"

Groppy exhaled and ran a hand through her loose braid. "I would rather you be with me in the woods than to be alone in the woods without me. At least I can protect you when I know where you are."

78

"Sorry," Nolan mumbled. Groppy nodded.

"I can keep looking through werewolf books in the library," Ava suggested. "I think I'm getting close to finding something that will help."

"I don't want to see the werewolf, again," Charlotte whispered. "It was too scary."

"You don't have to, Charlotte," Groppy said softly. "You were very brave tonight."

Charlotte didn't say anything, but she shook her head. She did not believe she had been brave.

"All right, to bed, everyone." Groppy yawned. "This old witch needs her beauty sleep." Ava noticed Nolan's mouth smirk with a laugh, and she swiftly smacked him on the arm. He winced and glared at her. The kids said their good nights and climbed the steps back to their bedroom. They were exhausted. As soon as their heads hit the pillow, their minds stopped racing and they instantly fell asleep.

* * *

The sun shone brightly through the bedroom window the next morning. Though they hadn't gotten much sleep, Ava hurriedly changed out of her pajamas, woke up Charlotte, told her where she was going, and dashed downstairs. After last night's encounter with the werewolf, she realized just how dangerous the magical animal was and was determined to find a way to trap it so no one else would get hurt. They would be leaving Groppy's in a few days, so technically they could just leave it alone. But Ava didn't like the idea of leaving Groppy to deal with this by herself. Ava was almost to the library door when she heard thundering steps behind her. She turned to see Nolan.

"Wait up!" he shouted as he skidded down the hall in his socks. He was still in his pajamas. "I want to help. Also, you forgot this." Nolan threw some cheese past the library door, and the hordes of cats that surrounded Ava jumped past her and for the smelly dairy. Ava was starting to grow used to the cats. She had nearly forgotten they were there.

She looked at him skeptically. "You know that there aren't any pictures in the books. It's all just words."

Nolan sighed. "I *can* read, ya know. I don't have to have pictures."

Ava squinted. "Who are you and what have you done with my brother?"

"Werewolves aren't the only animals that can change." Nolan smirked and sauntered ahead of his sister into the library.

* * *

Charlotte also stayed in her pajamas as she dragged herself downstairs to the kitchen and sat at the table by herself. She sighed deeply and rested her face in her hands. Groppy walked in the room dressed in her usual black with purple and green striped socks. Her raven hair had been washed and was held back in a nice tight braid. She gave her usual crooked grin as she saw Charlotte.

"Good morning, Charlotte. What would you like for breakfast?" Charlotte looked down at her hands. "I'm not hungry," she mumbled. Groppy pulled out a chair and joined Charlotte at the table.

"He's going to be all right," Groppy assured her. "Don't worry about Merlin."

"It's my fault. He's hurt because of me. Merlin was trying to save me because I was too scared and couldn't do anything but scream. I'm just too little."

Groppy shook her head. "Being little doesn't mean you can't do anything. Merlin is even smaller than you, and he was able to attack that big werewolf."

Charlotte looked up. "Wasn't he scared?"

Groppy nodded. "I'm sure he was. I bet he was even terrified. But there was something more important at that moment than fearing the werewolf."

"What's that?" Charlotte asked.

"Protecting you," Groppy answered sincerely. "You can find a lot of courage you didn't know you had when someone you care about is in trouble. And I know that same courage is inside of you, too." Charlotte gave a half-smile and nodded. Groppy smiled back. "So, how about some breakfast?"

"I'll have some chocolate cake," Charlotte answered. "Today is a good day for chocolate."

After breakfast, Groppy let the kids know that she was going to go into the woods to look for the tear in the magic realm. Ava and Nolan were still searching for answers in books, but Charlotte surprised them all by bravely asking to join Groppy in the woods. Groppy gladly accepted Charlotte's help and they headed outside. Charlotte was still spooked from the night before, but Groppy had reassured her that werewolves only come out at night and that she was perfectly safe with her during the day.

"You promise I won't see a werewolf?" Charlotte asked again, stopping at the edge of the yard in front of the forest.

"I promise," Groppy replied and held her warty hand to her heart. Charlotte closed her eyes and nodded, then boldly followed Groppy into the woods.

Now that it was daylight, it was much easier to see all the broken branches, low tree limbs, and hidden bushes that Charlotte hadn't been able to see the night before. Without a scary werewolf in sight and with the bright sun on her face, the walk through the woods was really quite nice. A few rabbits skittered across the forest floor past them.

"What are we looking for?" Charlotte asked Groppy as she stepped over a large tree root.

"The hole in the magic realm. I am guessing it will be close to the ground since I still think it was some pesky rabbit that chewed on the shield. The spell I cast places an invisible shield between their world and ours, but where the hole is, you should be able to see little sparkles—like glitter. Unfortunately, it's hard to see the sparkles in the daylight, but it's safer to search in the day. My eyes are old, and my back starts to hurt from bending over so much. Hopefully, your young eyes and smaller size will be able to spot the hole easily."

"Well, I'll try my hardest," Charlotte promised, and she crouched down close to the ground and began searching.

* * *

Nolan sat upside down in Groppy's chair in the library, his feet propped where his head should go, and his head where his legs should be. He slowly flipped through pages of another book, then groaned and dropped the open book on his face.

"I know I promised to help," he said to Ava, his voice muffled by the book over his mouth. "But this is a lot harder than I thought it would be. And these books have a lot of words. Like millions of words."

Ava sat on the floor, legs crossed, reading through another book, as well. Beside her lay a stack of fifteen or so other large old books that she had already flipped through. She sighed and rubbed the sides of her head. He was right. It was a lot of words. "Nolan, you don't have to keep reading."

"Oh, no," Nolan replied, trying to sound convincing. "I am thoroughly enjoying this. This is . . . great." Ava rolled her eyes and looked back down at her book, then pushed it away with a groan.

"You're right. This is impossible. I mean, Groppy couldn't even figure this out and she knows these books. Why did I think I could?" Ava leaned back until she lay flat on the floor, sprawled out like a starfish and sighed. "I give up."

Nolan rolled feet first off the chair. "You give up?" he reeled. "You never give up. You're like the number-one person to follow through on anything, even if it's awful chores Mom gives us or extra credit at school." Nolan walked over to his sister and stared down at her. "You are not a quitter, Ava. You're a fighter." He jabbed a pointed finger at her, and Ava's eyes widened. "You are going to get back up and read through those books and find a way to defeat that werewolf. And you want to know why? Because *you* are the only one who can. You're strong, and you're smart. Groppy needs you. She's too old to find the answer, Charlotte can't really read yet, and I'm *sick* of reading. So, get up and find it, Ava!"

Nolan's pep talk had startled Ava, but his eyes never wavered from hers. He had meant what he said. Ava didn't know what she was more shocked about. That her brother had tried to help her by reading a book, or the fact that he actually complimented her. But Nolan wasn't wrong. Ava got off the ground.

"You're right. I can find a way. I will help Groppy. But"—she turned toward her brother—"it's not because you can't. You just don't like reading."

"You got that right," Nolan said as he collapsed again in Groppy's chair. Ava looked around the book-strewn room.

"I keep looking through books that I think will help me, but none have," Ava thought out loud. "So maybe, I should look through a book that has nothing to do with werewolves."

Nolan shrugged. "It's worth a shot."

Ava reached out and grabbed a faded green and gold book with the title *Herbology Magic* and pulled it off the shelf. She flipped through the pages. Inside were detailed black and white pencil illustrations of wild plants and flowers that were known to the human realm and the magical realm. She scanned the book, reading different passages on witch hazel, thyme, rosemary, and red buds. Her eyes stopped on a section about a tree called Mountain Ash.

The Mountain Ash tree grows bright red berries, also known as Rowan berries. The berries are highly poisonous and can only be eaten if thoroughly cooked and made into a jam. Rowan berries can also be useful as a source of protection or barrier when dealing with magical creatures. If a magical creature walks into a circle of Rowan berries, they will be bound to the circle. But be careful—remove a single berry, and they will be set free.

Ava looked up from the book, ecstatic, with an excited and open smile.

Nolan sank further into the chair. "You're weirding me out."

"I found it!" Ava grinned from ear to ear. "I found a way to catch the werewolf."

∗   ∗   ∗

Charlotte's back and legs were aching from all the leaning over and squatting on the forest floor. She stood up and stretched for a few seconds then got back down and searched for the sparkly rip in the magical realm. She was determined to find it.

"Any luck, Charlotte?" Groppy called a few yards away.

"Not yet!" Charlotte yelled back. A bush rustled near her feet, and Charlotte jumped. Two brown bunnies stuck out their noses and cautiously sniffed the air.

"Oh." Charlotte laughed, relieved. "It's just some cute bunnies." The furry bunnies saw Charlotte and leaped out of the bush, running away from her.

"Wait!" she called to them. "Where are you going? I want to pet you!" Charlotte raced through the woods after the little creatures. They scampered swiftly across the forest floor. She did her best to keep up, but they were so fast. Charlotte had to stop to catch her breath and leaned against a tree. Dry leaves rustled near her foot. She looked down and just briefly saw the white fluff of a brown bunny's tail disappear into . . . nothing.

"What?" Charlotte looked around her. She saw the usual trees and forest, nothing out of the ordinary, but somehow the bunny had just disappeared. A few more dried leaves rustled near her, and Charlotte spotted the second bunny hopping past her. It followed the trail of the first and then mysteriously disappeared out of sight as well. Charlotte crouched down and looked where the small animal had gone. The sun shone brightly as she squinted and searched the ground. No bunnies. Just dead leaves and dirt.

As she searched, her shadow covered where the bunnies had disappeared, causing Charlotte to freeze. Sparkles appeared in her shadow. There was a curved arch of glimmer coming off the forest floor. She moved away and the sun hit the glittery tear in the realm, causing it to almost disappear.

"Aunt Poppy! Come quick! I think I found it!" she yelled excitedly. Groppy rushed over to Charlotte. Charlotte pointed with a thrilled expression on her face. "Look what happens when I stand right here." Charlotte blocked the sun's light with her body and the sparkly rip in the realm reappeared. Groppy hooted.

"You did it!" Groppy reached down and hugged Charlotte, then groaned and held her back. "You found it! I knew you could do it." She grimaced, rubbing her backside. "Now we just have to figure out how to get the wolf back through and then I can repair the shield." She scratched her chin. "Speaking of, I have to figure out how to do that, as well. Need something stronger this time."

"I can't wait to tell Nolan and Ava." Charlotte beamed.

Groppy tied a purple ribbon to the tree closest to the hole so it would be easier to find. Then she and Charlotte hurried back to the house. Charlotte burst through the front door, shouting, "I found it! I found the hole!" She jumped up and down. Ava and Nolan came running from the library.

"You did? That's amazing, Charlotte!" said Ava.

"Great work, squirt," Nolan added.

"We also found something," Ava said happily. "A way to trap the werewolf."

"Well, technically Ava found it," Nolan admitted. "But I was there for support." Ava nodded in agreement.

Groppy clapped her hands. "That is wonderful news, you two. I can't wait to hear what you found."

SCRATCH. SCRATCH. SCRATCH.

A small scratching sound emitted from down the hallway. They all turned their heads and looked. Nothing was there.

SCRATCH. SCRATCH. SCRATCH.

"Did something follow you inside?" asked Nolan.

Groppy tugged at her braid and peered down the darkened corridor. "I'm not sure. I don't believe so. We came in from the front door." The kids followed her toward the sound. The scratching continued and grew louder the closer they got to Groppy's bedroom door.

"Kids, get behind me. Just in case," Groppy said as she reached for the doorknob.

"Just in case, *what*?" Nolan asked, a little anxious, but Ava shushed him. Charlotte held on to her sister's hands and closed her eyes. The doorknob clicked and Groppy slowly opened the door. But she didn't yell. Instead, she exhaled in what seemed to be relief and joy. The kids looked up at her, puzzled.

"What is it?" Ava asked, still unsure. "Is it the werewolf?"

"No." Groppy shook her head. "But it's something for Charlotte." Charlotte squinted one eye open and peered at Groppy. "It's okay." Groppy motioned her forward.

Charlotte forced herself to let go of Ava's hand and took baby steps toward the half-open door. What she saw sitting inside Groppy's room made her gasp—a furry and healthy Merlin. Charlotte rushed forward, sliding to her knees so she could hug her friend.

"Took you long enough to find me," Merlin purred. Charlotte exhaled happily and held on tightly to her cat.

16

THAT EVENING AFTER DINNER, AVA EXPLAINED TO GROPPY ALL THE information she had found on trapping the werewolf.

"The book said it needed to be a complete circle of Mountain Ash or Rowan berries. Does that grow anywhere around here?" Ava asked Groppy while pointing to the pencil sketch in the herb book. Groppy scratched her chin.

"I have seen it in the woods. It's a red berry. I think we might have passed some today while looking for the tear. This is great research, Ava." Groppy applauded.

"Oh, it was nothing." Ava waved it off, but she was incredibly happy that her hours of searching had helped. "Now, we just need to think of something to put in the circle of berries to attract the werewolf to step inside."

"You can count me out," Merlin purred from where he sat by Charlotte. Charlotte had not stopped petting him all evening, and he thoroughly enjoyed the extra attention. Ava laughed.

"No, Merlin. I wasn't going to put you in there. Actually, I was thinking of Nolan." Ava gave a wicked smile and looked over at her brother. He was currently in the process of burping to make more room in his stomach for cookies. He belched triumphantly and glared over at his older sister.

"Sounds about right," Nolan mumbled and shoved another cookie into his mouth.

"But honestly, we do need something to get the wolf's attention," she continued. "I'm not sure what, though. Maybe something that he likes. He would smell it and track it down."

"Like cookies?" Charlotte asked. Ava shook her head.

"No, something that he would like to eat."

"Well, I like to eat cookies." Charlotte shrugged as she grabbed one off the plate near Nolan before he could stop her.

"Werewolves like fresh meat," Groppy said. "But I would hate to put an animal in there. Maybe a rabbit," she mumbled to herself.

"They like the smell of blood," Nolan commented while licking melted chocolate off his fingers. Ava's mouth twisted while Charlotte stuck out her tongue.

"That's yucky," Charlotte said.

"Did you read that somewhere?" Ava asked Nolan. He reached for another cookie before answering.

"Yeah, it was in one of those old books of Groppy's. Werewolves are attracted to the smell of blood." Instantly, Nolan tensed when he realized what he had said. Ava's eyes widened. There was a moment of silence before their great-aunt spoke with her now familiar, scratchy voice.

"Who is Groppy?"

The kids all looked at each other but remained silent. Ava subtly shook her head at the other two.

"That's what the children call you," Merlin answered. "It's a nickname. I think it suits you." He grinned. Ava shot Merlin a dirty look, but he just grinned even wider.

"Well, I don't know what to say." Groppy looked away briefly. Ava, Nolan, and Charlotte felt sick to their stomachs. They had given her that name because she had looked like a Groppy, and honestly, she still did, but they were starting to like her now. She really wasn't that bad. She might look terrifying at times on the outside, but inside, she was just a sweet old lady and a witch. Ava sputtered as she tried to explain but Groppy spoke first.

"Never in my entire life, which is long, have I ever been given a nickname." She smiled crookedly. "I love it."

The kids were shocked. If anything, Ava would have thought Groppy would have hated the nickname. But she loved it?

"Well, you look like a Groppy," Charlotte said silently. Groppy snorted.

"Yes, Charlotte, I agree. I do look like a Groppy."

Ava blinked in astonishment. She didn't know what else to say, so she turned back to Nolan to continue the conversation.

"So, you read that werewolves are attracted to blood?"

"Yep."

Ava cringed. "Where are we going to find blood?"

"Don't worry about that," Groppy said. "I've got plenty of that in vials upstairs. Is there one you want in particular?" she asked Nolan. "I have newt's blood, unicorn blood, bat blood, spider blood, pig's blood . . . "

"I think any blood will work," Nolan said. Ava held her stomach and tried not to toss the cookies she'd just eaten.

"Ya know, Groppy," said Nolan, "with all that blood, someone might think you're a vampire, too." Groppy looked over at Nolan and winked, which neither confirmed nor denied Nolan's thought. He grabbed the nearest blanket and covered up his throat, just in case. "Does anyone else feel cold?" he asked anxiously.

Ava was thinking out loud, "So, once we make the circle of berries, we'll pour some"—she shuddered—"blood into the circle. The werewolf will smell it and come looking for it. Once he finds it, he'll be stuck inside the circle of berries and will have to stay there till morning. And when the sun comes out, he'll turn back into a man, and Groppy can take him to the magic realm and fix the hole. And that's it. We figured it out!" she beamed.

"I'll be in the library tonight if you need me," Groppy said. "I think I may have found a new spell to fix the hole and make the shield stronger, but I need to read on it more."

"Sounds good." Ava nodded. "Tomorrow morning, we find the berries and tomorrow night . . . "

"We trap a werewolf," answered Groppy.

"Yes," Ava agreed. "We trap a werewolf."

* * *

The next morning, the kids, Merlin, and Groppy set out early into the woods, searching for the Mountain Ash tree with Rowan berries. They had a rough idea of how the tree looked from the sketch in the book, and they at least knew that the berries would be red. Unfortunately, there were quite a few plants that had red berries—holly bushes, red gooseberry bushes, nightshade, and winter berry, to name a few.

"It's too bad the berry couldn't have been literally any other color," Nolan complained, getting annoyed, "because there are only red berries in this forest."

"Keep looking, Nolan!" Ava shouted back at him as she foraged ahead, scanning the trees. "There has to be a Mountain Ash somewhere." But she was starting to grow concerned herself. It was a cloudy day and the wind blew swiftly, making the tree limbs dance. Dry leaves twirled in tiny tornadoes, and vines reached out and touched their legs as they continued their search through the thicket. Eventually, they needed a break, and each sat down to rest on the forest floor. Nolan sighed and leaned up against a tree, then slid to the ground

"Don't get discouraged," Groppy reassured the kids. "I know it's out here somewhere." Nolan rolled his eyes and absentmindedly picked at the small blades of grass growing near the roots of the tree, flicking them away. One hit Charlotte in the face.

"Hey!" she yelled. "That hurt." Nolan looked up, confused. "You hit me," she explained.

"It's just grass," Nolan said. "It couldn't hurt that much."

He looked down at the bits of clover and dried up weeds near his hand and noticed something round hidden beneath the grass—tiny little red berries. He must have picked one up by accident and flicked it at Charlotte. He leaned his head back and looked into the tree—more red berries.

"Um," Nolan pointed up. Ava followed his hand and gasped. The tree looked just like the one in the book.

"Rowan berries!" Ava shouted. Groppy looked up too and nodded.

"Yes! That's a Mountain Ash. Good work spotting that one, Nolan," Groppy said. Nolan knew that it was completely accidental that he even found the tree, but he took the praise just the same.

"Are there any more on the ground?" Ava asked, searching through the weeds. "I don't see many and we need a lot to make the circle."

"Looks like we'll have to get them from the tree," Groppy said.

"How?" Charlotte asked. "They're too high up."

"Too bad none of you have retractable claws that allow you to climb trees." Merlin yawned as he stretched and sharpened his claws on the trunk. They all stared at him impatiently. "Fine," he huffed, "I'll get the berries."

After they gathered the berries Merlin knocked down from the tree, they scouted out the perfect spot to place the trap. Ava felt it needed to be close to where they had seen the wolf the other night, while also being near large bushes or shrubs that they could hide behind. Groppy wanted to stay near the trap to make sure it worked, and the kids insisted on keeping her company.

Once they found the perfect spot, the children placed the berries in a wide circle, halfway burying them into the ground so that they wouldn't move. After setting up the trap, they all headed back to the house where they waited patiently and anxiously for the sun to set. As the day grew dark that evening, Groppy and the Alexander siblings ventured back to the trap set in the forest. Merlin did not join them. He had already had "enough fun in the woods" and happily stayed back at home, away from the danger.

It was two nights before Christmas, and instead of the normal family tradition of building a gingerbread house, Ava, Nolan, and Charlotte sat silently in the woods with Groppy, waiting on a blood-thirsty werewolf.

Once night fell, Groppy tiptoed from out behind the shrubbery over to the berry circle and poured a few drops of blood onto the dried leaves. *Splat. Splat. Splat.* She hurried back to the kids and crouched down.

"How long do you think it will take?" Ava whispered. The crisp night wind whipped at her hair and she tucked it behind her ears.

"Werewolves have a great sense of smell," Nolan answered. "They can smell blood from miles away. It shouldn't be long before . . . Did you hear that?" There was a rumbling, like the hum of train wheels on tracks, coming from the woods. Ava could feel the vibrations through her hands and knees as she crouched on the forest floor.

"Something is moving fast," she whispered and looked up at Groppy. The witch's eyes closed as she listened to sounds coming from the woods. The rumbling grew louder. The winter breeze turned into a rough gale, causing the branches of the bushes to shake and tug at their coats, making the group shiver. Ava anxiously watched the berries, hoping the wind wouldn't disturb them.

"He can smell it," Groppy said steadily. "He's coming."

Charlotte let out a whimper.

"It's all right." Ava squeezed her hand. "This time, we're with you. Nothing bad will happen." Ava smiled at her sister and turned her face back to the thundering sound. Her smile turned to a frown. She was quite afraid, but she didn't want Charlotte to see.

A mass of muscle and fur burst through the forest wall and hurdled toward the circle of berries. Charlotte let out a scream, but Nolan quickly covered her mouth. He bit his tongue so he wouldn't make a sound. Ava lost her voice. The werewolf was just as terrifying as the night before. Its teeth glimmered as it heaved breaths of air that turned to fog, its tongue lagging out the side of its mouth. Droplets of saliva fell to the ground as it came closer to the circle. To the kids' amazement, the beast jumped inside the berry ring and immediately began to lick up the blood. Ava trembled. They waited patiently and silently.

"Did it work?" Nolan whispered. Ava silenced him with her hand.

"Wait," she mouthed.

The werewolf licked the blood from the leaves and let out a snarl. There was no animal here for him to eat. He had been tricked. With one large paw he moved to step out of the circle but let out a piercing howl of pain that sent tingles up the children's spines. The circle of Rowan berries burned the werewolf's paw as he tried to cross. He sniffed the ground and let out another loud howl in frustration.

"He's caught," Nolan whispered both excited and terrified. "We did it!" The wind pressed on their backs pushing them into the bushes. Ava steadied herself.

"The weather is getting worse," she said to Groppy. "Should we go back?"

Groppy agreed. "It seems the berries have worked. But stay low. We don't want the werewolf to see us. He's angry. It would be better if we didn't leave all at once. We'd make less noise that way." Ava and Nolan looked at each other and nodded.

"We'll go first," Nolan said, pointing to Ava. "Groppy can stay hidden here with Charlotte and keep her safe."

"Be careful and silent as the grave," Groppy warned. "My magic won't work against him. If anything happens . . . "

"We'll figure something out," Ava said, trying to sound confident. Nolan gave his sister a questioning look, but she ignored it. "We'll have to."

Ava and Nolan crawled soundlessly away from the bushes and back on the trail toward Groppy's house. They did their best to stay on well-worn dirt paths to remain silent, avoiding crunchy dead leaves. Nolan stayed a few feet behind Ava and paused every so often to listen for movement from the wolf. The wind continued to howl, which helped to muffle some of their noise as they maneuvered around noisy underbrush. The wintry gale bit at their faces, and they zipped their coats up higher around their necks. Every so often, Ava glanced over her shoulder to make sure Nolan was still behind her. Finally, through the trees, Ava saw the soft candle glow from the window of Groppy's back room. They were almost to the edge of the forest. They were going to be okay.

A loud roaring sound swirled past the kids' ears. A tearing gust of wind nearly lifted them off their hands and feet, and they grabbed the earth and tree roots to steady themselves. Through the woods, they heard a loud howl and a shriek from a child.

"Charlotte!" Ava yelled. Nolan was already on his feet and running back through the forest to his little sister. Ava followed. What had seemed like miles crawling had only been a few hundred yards

Nolan reached the scene first. The blast of winter air had tossed the ring of berries, freeing the werewolf. Charlotte yelped in surprise, alerting the monster. Groppy quickly moved in front of Charlotte as the wolf stepped toward them. Nolan noticed a low branch on one of the pine trees behind them and hurriedly rushed toward his sister. Charlotte screamed when she felt hands on her shoulders then stopped when she saw Nolan's face.

"Climb the tree!" he shouted as he picked her up and placed her close to the low branch. She clung tightly to the bough and pulled herself up. Quickly, she spotted the next low limb and continued to climb with shaky arms and trembling legs, the adrenaline from fear giving her strength. Groppy grabbed a large fallen branch from the ground and swung it back and forth, wildly.

"Get back!" she yelled at the werewolf. The beast only seemed slightly troubled by her, but he kept moving forward. Ava froze, unsure of what to do, and stepped behind a pine tree a good distance from the scene. The wolf lashed out at Groppy and bit the tree limb, ripping it from her hands. It snapped in half between its sharp jaws.

"Oh, no," Ava whispered. She needed to do something. The wolf was going to attack Groppy and her siblings at any moment. But what could she do? Her mind raced and she desperately looked around for some help or ideas. Something grabbed her leg. She jerked and looked down to see a thorn bush that was stuck in her pants. She wrenched it free. But the bush gave her an idea. She shuddered at the thought but reached down with her left hand and pressed her index finger into a sharpened thorn. Ava sucked in a breath as the pain seared in her hand and a warm sticky liquid poured out. Bright red blood instantly appeared on the surface of her smooth hand. Grimacing, she took in a deep breath and let out a long howl to draw the wolf from her family.

The werewolf looked away from Groppy and Nolan. It lifted its ears and sniffed the air. The gray wolf began to drool and howled back into the wind. Following the scent of fresh blood, it left the others behind as it ripped through the forest straight toward Ava. Nolan looked to where the beast ran and was horrified to see his sister standing still.

"AVA, RUN!" Nolan screamed through the trees.

Ava started running. The wind whipped through her ears. Her tennis shoes slammed down on the forest floor, careful to avoid any fallen limb or tree roots. Her heart pounded loudly in her chest from terror and fatigue, but she pushed her legs to go faster. All she could hear was the thundering of paws across the fallen leaves coming closer and closer.

17

AVA NEVER THOUGHT SHE WOULD EVER BE SO HAPPY TO SEE GROPPY'S crooked house, but a little hope crept back in her as she broke through the tree line and raced toward the webbed covered home. It was the fastest she had ever run in her life. Her feet pounded on the tall dead grass as she flew to the front porch. The werewolf was swiftly gaining on her.

Ava hurdled over the creaky old steps and burst through the front door. With tremoring hands, she locked all the locks and bolts and then stumbled over her feet as she frantically scampered up the stairs. She wasn't three steps up when she heard a loud BANG at the door. The wolf was trying to get in.

* * *

"What can we do?" Nolan looked at Groppy, frantic. "He'll kill her!" Groppy, Nolan, and Charlotte were too slow to stop the werewolf and stood helpless in the woods.

"Take my hand," Groppy instructed as both Charlotte and Nolan latched on to her. She pulled out a vial of purple potion from her pocket. "There was just a drop left in the cauldron. It will be enough to get us back to the house. We'll never get there in time on foot." The children felt the same strange tingling feeling on their skin and closed their eyes. Just like last time, when their eyes reopened, they were in their great-aunt's house. This time, in Groppy's bedroom. Groppy sniffed the air and listened.

"Ava's here. She's upstairs in the bedroom."

"You can smell her?" Nolan questioned.

94

"I'm a witch, Nolan," Groppy answered as an obvious explanation.

Nolan shrugged. A tail brushed across his pant leg and he jumped. "Wolf!"

"Shhh," Groppy shushed him. "It's just the cats."

The lights were off, so neither Nolan nor Charlotte had noticed the hundreds of cats hiding out in Groppy's room. Charlotte moved in closer to her aunt.

"Is the wolf inside the house, too?" she whispered.

Groppy placed her ear on the door and listened.

BOOM!

The front door of the house fell inward and slammed onto the wooden floor, sending bolts and screws scattering.

"That would be a *yes*," Nolan answered, eyes wide.

"We need to get to Ava." Groppy tugged at her braid, trying to think.

"Can't you wish the werewolf away?" Nolan suggested.

Groppy shook her head. "No, my magic does not work on werewolves, remember?"

"Oh, right." Nolan bit his lip. Charlotte was trembling. She looked to Groppy and Nolan and knew they would eventually think of something. But no one had any ideas. They needed a plan, and fast. Ava's life depended on it.

Suddenly, an idea popped into Charlotte's head. Maybe that would work. But, no. Groppy and Nolan would think of something better; she just needed to wait. The seconds ticked by and nobody said anything. Time was running out. The werewolf continued to tear up the house, throwing furniture aside. Charlotte wrung her hands. The wolf turned over something large in the kitchen. It hit the floor with a *BANG* and made Charlotte's heart nearly jump out of her chest.

"I have an idea!" she yipped. The other two looked at her surprised. "I . . . " she began but stopped and looked away.

"Go on, Charlotte," Nolan encouraged. "What's your idea?"

"Well," she said as she looked at the floor and then back at them. "Groppy, you said Ava was in the bedroom and we're in your room. Since both the doors are magical, we could go through your door to the secret stairs and get Ava and bring her back here so she's not out there alone with the wolf."

Charlotte waited for Nolan to say it was a terrible idea. But he didn't. "That's actually a pretty good plan. Why didn't I think of that?" Nolan said.

"Excellent, Charlotte," Groppy agreed. "Let's go. Now!" Groppy switched the doorknob and was about to open the door when Charlotte stopped her.

"Wait!" Charlotte cried out. "Just me. I need to go alone. You need to stay here in case the wolf does come to your room. You're stronger together, and you have to keep this door shut. Ava and I will be safe on the hidden stairs. If the wolf gets through your door, we won't be able to get back."

Nolan looked at Groppy anxiously and then back to Charlotte. Nolan spoke first. "No, you can't go by yourself."

"I have to." Charlotte's voice was shaky but firm. "I am afraid, but saving Ava is more important than being afraid."

Groppy understood. "Courage," said Groppy. Charlotte looked up at her and nodded. "Go ahead, Charlotte. Just think of your bedroom, and the red door will appear on the stairs. But be quick!"

Before Nolan could protest, Charlotte was through the door and gone.

Nolan's mouth dropped as he gaped up at Groppy. "You let her go alone?"

"She can do this," Groppy answered firmly. "I believe in her."

Nolan stared anxiously at the closed door. "Be brave, Charlotte," he whispered. "I believe in you."

* * *

Ava laid underneath the blankets of her bed, covered in pillows. Her breath came in quick gasps. She had run up the stairs, into the bedroom, and locked all the doors before she jumped into her bed to hide. As she lay there quietly, something moved by her feet. Ava let out a sharp shriek.

"Hush, it will hear you," a voice hissed. Ava lifted the bed covers off her head. "Merlin?" her voice quivered.

"I stay back home where it's safe and you bring the danger here. Unbelievable," Merlin spat as he walked across her stomach and toward Ava's face. "So, what's your plan now?"

"Try not to get eaten," Ava squeaked. She felt a little better now that she wasn't alone. "Do you know where the others are?" she asked the cat, hopeful.

Merlin shook his head. "Not a clue." Ava's heart sank. A doorknob rattled, and Ava nearly fell out of the bed. Merlin *rawred* and crawled underneath the covers with her. Her whole body shook, and she closed her eyes tight, knowing that the wolf would easily see her. She hoped he wouldn't notice the shaking lump under the bedsheets, but she couldn't kid herself. This was it.

"Ava," a small voice whispered through the open door. Ava knew that voice and nearly cried.

"Charlotte!" Ava rasped as she sat up from the bed. Her little sister smiled when she saw Ava still alive and safe. "Charlotte, what are you doing here? Where is Groppy?"

"No time to explain," Charlotte said. "Come with me. We can go back to Groppy's room through here. Everyone else is there, too."

"I'm not there," Merlin meowed.

"Merlin!" Charlotte quickly reached down and pet the cat. "You're okay!" Merlin purred.

Ava quickly got off the bed and headed toward the door. A crash sounded nearby as an owl portrait fell off the wall. The glass shattered into pieces and trickled down the stairs. Ava and Charlotte stiffened. A loud snarl followed by heavy footsteps sounded on the balcony.

"Werewolf," they both mouthed silently to each other. Ava closed the door leading to Nolan's room, changed the knobs, and pushed Charlotte through to the hidden staircase with Merlin close behind. Charlotte was beginning to feel relief. Her plan was going to work. Ava went to close the door when suddenly she stopped. She had realized something awful.

"Charlotte," she whispered swiftly. "If we go through this door, the wolf will just follow us, and we will put everyone in danger. We don't have anyone to change the doorknob back."

"What?" Charlotte didn't understand and they didn't have the time. The wolf was headed for their bedroom.

THUD. THUD. THUD.

"The doorknob will *still* be on the right side. The wolf will just see we're not in the bedroom and go through Nolan's door, right to where we are in the stairwell. If he doesn't catch us and eat us first, he'll just follow us to Groppy's room!"

Charlotte's eyes widened. "Oh, no, no, no." She shook her head. Her idea wasn't going to work, and she had made everything worse. Ava closed the door and changed the knob back.

BANG. BANG. BANG.

The werewolf pounded on the outside door. The hinges creaked as they began to tear away from the door frame. At any moment, the wolf would have them. Ava turned to Charlotte.

"Go into Nolan's room and take Merlin with you. I'll quickly change the doorknob and sneak out the window. Hopefully, once the wolf breaks in, he'll go through the door and into the stairwell. Then I'll find a way to warn Groppy so she doesn't open her door to the werewolf."

"No! You won't be fast enough," Charlotte protested. "And you can't fit through the window. You're too big. You'd never fit." Charlotte looked over at the window and then at her own self. "I'm little. You go through this door with Merlin and I'll switch the knobs and go out the window."

"Charlotte, no, I can't let you . . . "

"Yes, you can," Charlotte interrupted. "You have to trust me, Ava. Please."

Ava didn't know what made her nod her head. "Okay." But there was something in her little sister's eyes that made her believe. She would have to trust her.

BANG. BANG. BANG.

"Go now!" Charlotte yelled. She pushed her sister through the door frame and slammed it shut, changing the knobs. Ava was left alone in Nolan's room.

Charlotte raced to the window and tugged. It was stuck. "No," she exhaled, horrified. Frantically, she pulled harder, but the frame wouldn't budge. Panic set in. Something brushed against her leg. She yelped and looked down. "Merlin! You were supposed to go with Ava."

Merlin twitched his tail. "And leave you alone? I don't think so. Quick. Under the bed!" Charlotte scrambled and crawled beneath the bed. She pulled the covers down to the floor to hide herself and Merlin. Charlotte held the cat close as the bedroom door crashed to the floor. The werewolf was in the room.

She tried to hold her breath, but she couldn't stop her little heart that beat rapidly in her chest. Charlotte watched the furry paws with large claws walk across the black shag rug. The wolf breathed in deeply.

Charlotte looked down at Merlin in her arms. He was a shaking ball of fur. She looked back at the door frame to her room. It was a wide-open hole, the red door lying down in the hallway. Wait. Open doors.

Charlotte closed her eyes and tried to think of when Nolan first told them about the secret stairwell. He had gotten stuck on the staircase between the doors because Ava had left his door *open*. Charlotte's eyes opened. *You can't go through an open door.* She pulled Merlin up to her face and whispered in his ear. He nodded. The wolf stopped and sniffed the air again. Charlotte stilled and watched in horror as its paws turned toward her bed. Merlin kicked against her body in fear. His clawed paw stuck Charlotte in the leg. She sucked in her breath. The claws stung, and she slid a hand down and rubbed where they sank in her skin. She felt something in her pocket. Cheese. Stinky blue cheese. Quickly, Charlotte reached in, grabbed a piece of cheese, and hurled it as hard as she could, underneath Nolan's bedroom door.

The werewolf smelled the food and lunged for it, drooling. The cheese disappeared under the gap below the door and the beast snarled. It bit the doorknob, tearing at it with his jaws. As the door swung open, the wolf rushed inside. Merlin raced out from under the bed and headed toward the balcony. Scrambling, Charlotte crawled out and threw herself at the red door. The wolf turned and reached for her, but it was too late. Its paw slammed against the closed door. Charlotte quickly pulled the doorknob out and held it to her chest. She leaned against the door. Her heart was racing. The werewolf was on the wooden stairs.

Charlotte took a few deep breaths as she leaned against the closed red door. Hopefully, Merlin got to Groppy in time. She steadied herself and placed the golden knob back on the left side, trapping the wolf in the stairwell, and opened the door to Nolan's bedroom.

* * *

Ava held on tightly to Nolan's pillow and breathed steadily into it. It seemed like hours since Charlotte had shoved her through the door frame. Ava had heard their bedroom door crash to the floor and wanted to rush to her sister, but she had promised Charlotte that she would trust her. So, she waited and waited, growing ever anxious.

What if something went wrong? What if Charlotte couldn't get out the window in time? How long was Ava supposed to wait in here? What if the werewolf got Charlotte? What if it went back downstairs and got Groppy and Nolan, too? What if? What if? WHAT IF?

The doorknob twisted. Ava sank back against the bed, her eyes glued on the door. What was going to come through it, she didn't know, and she didn't have time to think, but she kept her eyes open. She would face whatever it was.

Tight brown curls fell past the frame as a small head peeked in. Bright eyes darted around the room until they fell on Ava. Both Charlotte and Ava let out a huge sigh as they saw each other. Charlotte raced to her sister and they held on tightly to one another.

"Did it work?" Ava asked into her sister's hair. Charlotte nodded.

"But . . . " Charlotte looked up and winced. "It almost didn't." Ava jerked her head toward Charlotte's, and her little sister quickly explained what happened in their bedroom.

"But won't the wolf go to Groppy now that it's on the hidden stairs?" Ava asked, troubled. Charlotte shook her head.

"No, I told Merlin to have Groppy open her bedroom door. The wolf can't walk through an open door, remember? Both of our doors are open." She looked toward their room. "And our bedroom door is on the floor. The wolf is stuck on the steps. We're safe." She exhaled. Ava blinked, astonished.

"And you came up with all of that while stuck under the bed?" she asked, dumbfounded.

"Yep." Charlotte beamed. Ava hugged Charlotte tighter. "I couldn't have thought of that. I would have been too terrified. You're so brave."

Charlotte buried her face into her sister's shoulder. "Groppy said that people find courage when someone they care about is in trouble." Ava smiled, and they stayed close to each other until Merlin, Nolan, and Groppy found them. They were safe, too. Merlin reached them in time. Everyone had survived and it was all thanks to Charlotte.

18

THAT NIGHT, THE ALEXANDER CHILDREN CAMPED OUT IN GROPPY'S room in sleeping bags on the floor near her bed. There was no way they were sleeping in their rooms tonight. Even with the werewolf safely trapped on the stairwell, there was *still* a werewolf trapped on the stairwell. Groppy cast a transparency spell so the kids could see the bright winter night sky through the ceiling. The twinkling stars were a constant night light. Merlin curled up on Charlotte's sleeping bag. They reminisced on all the crazy things that had happened that week. Groppy and Nolan applauded Charlotte and Ava for their quick thinking and especially Charlotte for her courage. They soon grew tired from talking and crawled into their sleeping bags. It had been a long week, but at last, the three kids finally felt safe and fell asleep.

* * *

The next morning was Christmas Eve. They would have completely forgotten had it not been for Charlotte.

"It's Christmas Eve!" Charlotte exclaimed. Nolan moaned and attempted to throw a pillow at his sister, but he missed. She was moving too much. "Santa comes tonight!"

"Could you go be happy in another room?" Nolan said, face down in his pillow. Charlotte giggled and skipped out and down the hall.

Ava rubbed her eyes and yawned. It was like Charlotte had completely forgotten about last night's terrors when there was the promise of presents.

"Actually," said Groppy, "I was meaning to ask you kids what you do for Christmas. I've never really done much for the holiday. Well . . . " She thought about it. "Usually no one comes over. Just me and the cats."

"It's a lot of fun," said Merlin. Ava caught his sarcasm.

"We decorate a gingerbread house," Ava answered while she stretched. "Watch movies. Go see lights."

"Mom lets us stay in pajamas on the couch and bakes us whatever we want," added Nolan.

Groppy looked over at Nolan and leaned her head to the side. "I highly doubt that."

"Worth a shot." Nolan shrugged.

"That sounds like fun. But"—Groppy scratched her head—"I don't think I have anything to make a gingerbread house, or movies to watch, and there's no one around us for miles. Especially not anyone with lights. I can at least go get some supplies for the gingerbread."

"Can't you just make one with magic?" Nolan's muffled voice spoke from the pillow.

Groppy nodded. "I could, yes, but I want to make one with all of you, without magic. I've been so busy with the wolf issue, I haven't been able to spend time with you, and you leave tomorrow."

"Tomorrow!" Ava groaned. "Aww, has it been a week already?" Even as she said it, Ava realized how much her thoughts had changed from the first day she arrived.

"It's gone by quick." Groppy sighed. "But we will enjoy the time we have left. Come on, let's eat some breakfast." She headed for the open door and turned back as she remembered, "And afterwards, I need to take care of a werewolf."

* * *

"Are you sure he's changed?" asked Charlotte nervously. They were all back in Groppy's room and about to enter the secret stairwell.

"Positive," Groppy nodded. "But just stay behind me. Better safe than sorry."

The witch changed the doorknob and opened the door. The stairwell was empty. The only movements were the candles that flickered on the walls.

"Hello!" Groppy called out with her creaky voice.

"Heellloooo!" a low voice answered back.

"Was that a howl?" Ava asked, taking a step back down the stairs.

"No," said Nolan. "I think that was a long hello. Right, Groppy?"

"Yes," she nodded. "He's not a wolf now."

Something stirred in the shadows and began to move slowly down the stairs with heavy, uneven steps. The kids all tensed and pushed closer to their great-aunt. As the creature came nearer, its features became clearer.

"It's a hairy man!" yelled Charlotte.

"What in the world?" Nolan commented, bewildered. The kids gaped as a man with long gray hair, furry knuckles, and thick black sideburns gazed at them with veiny red eyes. He wore a tattered shirt and jeans and no socks or shoes.

Groppy shook her head. "Out of all the wolves . . . Ava, Nolan, Charlotte, this is Lucien. Lucien, these are my great-nieces and nephew whom you nearly ate last night."

The shaggy man flinched with guilt. He scratched his head and a few pieces of dirt and dried blood fell onto the steps. "I am very sorry," he said. His voice was muffled by a mouth full of sharpened human teeth. "I was out looking for food one night and I noticed the tear in the realm. I hadn't had a taste of rabbit in ages. I couldn't help myself. Then my werewolf self wouldn't let me change back to human. I've been wandering in the woods ever since." Ava noticed that he rubbed at a red mark on his hand. That must have been where the Rowan berries burned it when it was a paw. "I'm guessing you captured me. Honestly, thank you."

"Well, you should thank the kids. They were the smart ones to figure it out," Groppy admonished. The wolf man looked down at the children and somewhat smiled, showing his fangs. "Thank you."

The kids all nodded.

"This is weird," Nolan whispered to Ava.

"All right, let's get you back inside the realm and get that hole fixed," Groppy said as she patted the hairy man's shoulder. "I found a spell that not even a rabbit can nibble on." She opened the door to the hallway and led Lucien out of the house and back into the woods.

"So, Groppy is friends with a werewolf? She just keeps getting cooler." Nolan laughed.

"It's so odd," Ava said. "I mean, last night we were running for our lives from a werewolf, and today he is just a hairy man with decent manners. Groppy has a very interesting life."

"You have no idea." Merlin stretched.

"Do you know Lucien?" Ava asked the cat.

"Yes, I do. I thought I recognized his scent earlier. He used to be a powerful wizard. Then he was bitten by a werewolf and hasn't had much control of his powers since."

"Poor Lucien." Charlotte frowned.

"Wait," Nolan said, "I thought Groppy said she was the only witch around here."

"She is." Merlin nodded. "There was Lucien, and then another even more powerful wizard that lived near the woods. But now it's just Groppy."

"Who was the other powerful wizard?" Ava asked.

Merlin flicked his tail. "I forget. You'll have to ask Groppy when she gets back."

"Hmm. I have a feeling she has even more secrets we don't know about," Nolan said.

"Maybe we should try to come here more often and keep Groppy company," Charlotte suggested.

"I think that sounds like a pretty good idea," Ava agreed.

* * *

Once the wolf business was taken care of and the tear in the shield fixed and reinforced with a new spell, Groppy headed out to get supplies for making gingerbread while the kids got ready for the day.

Ava was folding up her sleeping bag and thinking out loud. "Did you hear Groppy say she never really celebrated Christmas?" Charlotte nodded while she pulled on her socks. Mom had packed her holiday socks with green and red stripes. She snorted, as they reminded her of Groppy.

"Yeah," Nolan answered. He had managed to get himself out of his pajamas, but that was as far as he'd gotten. He lay on his bed, too full of pancakes from breakfast.

"Well, don't you think that's sad?" Ava asked.

"That's probably why her house doesn't look like Christmas," Charlotte commented. "She doesn't have any Christmasy stuff to put up."

"That's it!" Ava turned to face her sister who had put on her sweater with a painted handprint reindeer. "We can decorate a tree and surprise Groppy with it."

"But she doesn't have a tree," Nolan pointed out.

Ava shook her head. "We are literally by the woods. We can go get a small tree and bring it back here."

"Yay!" Charlotte clapped her hands. Nolan sighed and rolled off the bed. It looked like he would have to get dressed after all.

* * *

The kids found a small pine tree right at the edge of the woods. It was almost as tall as Ava. After a lot of pushing and bending, the tiny trunk finally snapped, and the kids hauled the tree back inside and leaned it against the wall. Ava wiped the dirt from her hands on her pants.

"Now to decorate it."

"But with what?" Charlotte looked around. "We don't have any ornaments."

"We'll just have to be creative," Ava replied as she looked around. "We need something for tinsel."

"How about all those spiderwebs on her house? I bet we could stretch those out as tinsel," Nolan half-joked.

"That actually might work." Ava nodded. "Yeah, let's try that."

Nolan looked disgusted. "I wasn't serious."

While Nolan and Ava grabbed sticky webbing from off the house, Charlotte looked around for ornaments.

"What do you think, Merlin?" she asked the cat who was close at her feet.

"I know where the cats all puke their hairballs. You could hang those. They are round like ornaments." The cat smiled back.

"Gross!" Charlotte stuck her tongue out. "We are not using those."

"Then I'm out of ideas."

Charlotte glared at Merlin. "You're not being very helpful," she huffed. Merlin purred and Charlotte softened. "Ugh. I can never stay mad at you."

She picked him up and carried him into the kitchen. "Maybe something in here will work." She looked around the cabinets and in drawers, but nothing stood out. Then she looked in the fridge and spotted a plate of chocolate spiders. "The surprise turnovers!" she gasped. We can hang the leftover spiders from the turnovers on the tree. They will match the webs."

Merlin flicked his tail. "Sounds good to me."

Nolan and Ava came back inside, their hands full and sticky of wound web, and started draping it around the tree as Charlotte hung the spiders.

"We need some lights," Nolan commented as he tried to pull the webbing out of his hair and face. "All Groppy has is candles."

"I've read that in some countries, people put small candles in their Christmas trees for lights," Ava informed them while also trying to get webbing out of her hair.

Nolan looked at her skeptically. "Well, then they must be really careful."

"That doesn't sound like us." Charlotte giggled.

"You're right," Ava said. "Maybe Groppy can help us there." The siblings finished decorating and took a step back to look at their creation. "Well, it's a different-looking Christmas tree, but this is a different-looking Christmas."

Nolan shrugged. "Works for me."

"I think it looks nice." Ava smiled. "It's a Groppy tree. She'll love it."

"Yeah." Charlotte smiled. "A Groppy tree."

* * *

Groppy returned with the gingerbread supplies. She loved the tree and had an idea for the lights. The kids strung some popcorn on a string, and as Groppy touched each puffed kernel, it let off a purple glow. They wrapped the glowing popcorn lights around the tree. It was perfect. Everything was done with a touch of "Groppy"—the tree, decorations, and even the gingerbread house they made to look like their great-aunt's home.

"It looks like a haunted house," remarked Nolan as they sat at the kitchen table, eating from the leftover bags of icing and gingerbread pieces. "But your house isn't haunted, right, Groppy?" Nolan asked suspiciously. Groppy only smiled and continued to hum as she added the black icing to outline the crooked shutters. Nolan sighed and went back to adding gummy bats around the chimney.

As Ava, Nolan, and Charlotte walked back to Groppy's room that night, they had mixed emotions. They were excited that tomorrow was Christmas, but they were also very sad. It would be their last day with Groppy, her creepy cat-filled house, and magical woods. They snuggled in their warm beds as Merlin snored soundly on top of Charlotte's sleeping bag.

"Groppy?" Ava asked.

"Yes."

"Merlin told us about how you knew Lucien. That he used to be a wizard, but then he got bitten by a werewolf."

Groppy sighed. "Yes, he was a good wizard, too. He loved the animals. He was always out in the magical realm taking notes on the magical creatures and helping them, kind of like a veterinarian. He tended to the animals' wounds and documented new things he found out about them. I told him he needed to be careful, but he said I worried too much."

"And that's how he got bitten?" Charlotte asked. "He wasn't careful?"

"Yes." Groppy nodded. "A werewolf had injured its leg, and while Lucien was tending to it, the werewolf bit him. Now he just stays in the realm since he can't control his powers anymore. He's harmless as you saw. Well, when he's not a werewolf."

"Merlin also mentioned that there was another wizard that used to live here," Nolan said.

Groppy raised an eyebrow. "He did, did he?"

"Yes, and he said that wizard was even more powerful than Lucien."

Groppy snorted. "Powerful? I would have said mischievous."

"Merlin said you could tell us about him," said Ava. "Where is the wizard now?"

Groppy leaned in closer to the kids. "He's in this room." They leaned back in their sleeping bags, startled.

"Where?" Charlotte asked.

Ava pulled her sleeping bag up around her and scooted closer to Groppy's bed. Nolan looked around the room. There was no one else in here, except Merlin. Then he remembered when he first met Merlin and the cat stared at him with those bright hazel eyes.

"It's Merlin!" Nolan pointed to the sleeping cat.

Groppy nodded. "You are correct."

"Wait a minute," Ava said as she thought about the snowstorm in the living room. "He didn't do any magic when we were stuck in the snow."

"He can't," said Groppy. "I made sure of that. Merlin is an old friend of mine. He was a pretty good wizard, but he liked to cause mischief."

"Did he do something bad?" asked Charlotte.

"No, not really." Groppy shook her head. "He just liked to play jokes on people. They were mostly harmless, more so annoying. But then one day he played a joke on the wrong person, a very all-powerful witch, and she was not happy."

"What happened?" Nolan asked.

"Well for one, he broke her heart."

"Aww," Charlotte said.

"And then he wanted to leave her castle with a bang, and he miscalculated the spell. Kind of blew the whole thing up."

"Oh no!" Ava put her hand to her mouth.

"He was in big trouble and needed to hide. So, he came to his best friend, me, to help him. I thought he deserved whatever punishment she wanted to deal him, but in the end, I helped him hide out as a cat. We used our combined powers, turned him into a cat, and he camouflaged quite well here among all the other cats."

"And the witch can't find him?" Ava asked.

"That's why we combined our powers," Groppy explained. "We enchanted the spell so he could not be detected by any witch or wizard. He just has to not talk when and if someone comes around. Which seems to be difficult for him."

"And what about his powers?" Nolan asked.

Groppy smirked. "I took care of that. He was supposed to still have his powers after the cat transformation, but as long as he was living with me, I didn't want to deal with any of his mischief. I knew he hadn't learned his lesson. So, when we enchanted the spell, I secretly added another charm that makes it impossible for him to use his magic as a cat. So, if he stays hiding out as a cat, he has no powers."

"Poor Merlin." Charlotte stroked his head.

"Poor Merlin my foot," Groppy huffed. "True to form, he still finds a way to cause mischief, even as a cat. He coughs up hairballs in my kitchen, goes up to the spell room and knocks my vials off the table and shelves, breaking them, and two weeks ago, he pushed all the cats' litter boxes into my room." Groppy shuddered. "It smelled for days. That's why he got punished and kicked out of the house. I've been trying to rid my room of kitty litter stench. Then your mom called and asked if I could watch you, and I got excited and forgot about Merlin. And soon after, the werewolf showed up."

"I let Merlin back in the house," Nolan admitted.

"Oh, that's all right," Groppy said. "I had planned on letting him back in the next day." She looked down at Merlin and smiled. "He's been very well behaved around you. Stinky cat."

Charlotte nuzzled her nose against Merlin's head then yawned.

"Yes, it's time for bed," Groppy said as she leaned back into her bed. "Good night, children."

"Good night, Groppy," they returned, and then snuggled back into their sleeping bags and quickly fell asleep.

* * *

"PRESENTS!" Charlotte shouted from down the hall. Nolan and Ava rubbed their eyes as they stumbled into the living room where the tree sat. Underneath lay a pile of gifts for each of them. Obviously, their mom had remembered to tell Santa where they would be. The kids tore into the gifts excitedly. There was even a present for Groppy—a pointed black hat with a wide brim.

"How did Santa know I lost mine?" Groppy grinned as she donned the new hat. It completed her witch outfit. How could anyone not think she was a witch? The kids would never know. A knock sounded at the door and everyone froze. Last time there was pounding at the door, it was a werewolf. But he was safely back in the magic realm. Right? The kids cautiously peeked down the foyer. Another loud knock sounded.

"Aunt Poppy! Kids! Are you awake?"

"It's Mom!" Charlotte jumped up and ran to the door. She opened it and leaped into her mother's arms. Nolan and Ava raced over as well to hug their parents. Dad was bringing in food from the car. "How about Chinese takeout for a traditional Christmas lunch?" He laughed and added, "It was the only restaurant still open."

"I have it every Christmas," Groppy said. "I hope you got extra egg rolls."

As the family sat and ate at the table, enjoying their Christmas lunch, they all shared their week's experiences.

"The hospital was swamped, but fortunately we had enough beds for everyone. We were so grateful that we were able to leave so we could spend the holiday with our family," Mom said happily while looking at Ava, Nolan, Charlotte, and Groppy. Dad nodded.

"We were lucky," he said while reaching for another egg roll.

"So, how was your week?" Mom asked. Nolan was about to shove a forkful of noodles in his mouth but stopped and looked at Ava, who had also stopped chewing her sesame chicken.

"We caught a werewolf!" Charlotte exclaimed. A few pieces of rice fell out of her mouth and on the table.

"Oh?" Mom questioned. Ava grimaced.

"Yes, we caught it, and I got a pony, but it disappeared. Then it snowed inside the house. It was terrifying but then so much fun."

"Well, it sounds like you had a great time," Dad said between bites of his egg roll. "Thank you again, Aunt Poppy, for watching them. Looks like they had a lot of fun."

Ava looked around, confused. Charlotte had just told them everything that had happened that week, and their parents hadn't even questioned it. It was almost like her parents didn't believe it. Ava glanced over at Nolan, who shrugged and continued eating. Mom looked over at Ava.

"Did you have fun too, sweetheart?" she asked.

"Um, yes," Ava answered, a little muddled. "I really did."

"Same here," Nolan added with a mouth full of sesame chicken.

* * *

That afternoon, Ava walked out onto the now familiar web-covered front porch and sat down on a creaky step. She rested her elbows on her knees, put her head in her hands, and sighed. A light breeze rustled the trees and pushed fallen leaves across the yellowed grass. She was all packed up, and they were about to leave to go home. She frowned and sighed again more deeply. She now realized how much she had enjoyed being here with Groppy.

The door shut behind her and footsteps thudded across the porch to the front step. Ava looked down and saw a pair of pointed black shoes.

"Ava, what's wrong?" Groppy sat down on the steps beside her.

"I don't want to leave. I had so much fun with you. And even if at times it was horrifying and I almost died, it was amazing . . . magical."

Groppy grinned her usual crooked grin. "I am so glad to hear it! I was afraid I had ruined your vacation," she said, relieved. "Not everyone gets chased by a werewolf or nearly frozen to death in a house blizzard."

"Yeah," Ava snorted. "And about that . . . Mom and Dad don't believe it. Any of it."

"Well, Ava, it's magic. And for some people, it's hard to believe that it exists. But it does. And not everyone will believe you, but that's okay. You know it's true, and that's all that matters."

"But doesn't it bother you that people just think you're crazy and dress up like a witch? If they knew you were an actual witch and that magic was real, they wouldn't think anything of it."

Groppy thought about that and inclined her head toward Ava. "Ava, I am always honest about who I am regardless of what people may think. And maybe not dressing like a witch would keep people from staring at me, but then it wouldn't be me. You should never hide who you are. No matter what people may think or won't believe." Ava thought about this and slowly nodded. She understood. Groppy was Groppy, and no one was going to change that.

"Besides, if anyone is too mean, I can just turn them into a toad." Groppy cackled.

Ava smiled. "Wait." She froze and looked at her great-aunt. "There are a lot of toads around your house. I hear them croaking every night." Groppy just smiled and kept on laughing. Ava shook her head and laughed too.

* * *

Mom and Dad packed the suitcases into the car as the kids all hugged Groppy goodbye. Ava held on to her the longest and breathed in the now dear smell of strong spices. Charlotte kissed Merlin on the head and told him she would be back soon.

"You better," he purred. "Don't leave me alone with this old witch." Charlotte giggled and pet him again, then headed to the car.

"You may be a Groppy, but you're the best one ever," Nolan said as he gave his great-aunt one last hug.

"I'm the *only* Groppy, Nolan." She winked. He winked back and jumped off the steps.

"We promise to come back soon, Groppy. Real soon," Ava said. She wiped her eyes quickly so Groppy wouldn't see any tears.

"I know you will." Groppy beamed.

Ava stepped down off the porch, then turned back. "Groppy, the real reason we started calling you that was because we were afraid of you. We were wrong. We just didn't know you. I'm sorry."

Groppy grinned and reached out for Ava's hand and squeezed it. "Oh, I know. But I still love the name, just the same."

Ava smiled. "Okay. Well, goodbye, Groppy."

"Goodbye, Ava." Groppy smiled back.

As the car left the gravel driveway, the kids all looked out the window at the old leaning house with chipped paint, cobwebs, and a crooked chimney that puffed smoke. Tall dead grass and weeds covered the yard as a cool breeze swayed what few leaves were left on the skeletal trees around the house. The woods in the background were still deep, thick, and dark, full of magical creatures, and the forest cast a ghostly shadow over the yard. But that house was now a second home full of magic and mystery. And even better, inside was a talking cat and Groppy. The Alexander children all smiled. They most definitely would be coming back.

ABOUT THE AUTHOR

Born in a small town in Alabama, Hallie Christensen grew up in a home filled with books and frequent trips to the library. She attended young authors' conferences while in elementary school and enjoyed writing her own stories and sharing them with others. She received her BA in English with a minor in Italian while attending the University of Alabama and marching in the Million Dollar Band. After graduating, she worked at a library while she obtained her MA in teaching English from Faulkner University. She now teaches English courses at a community college and lives in northern Alabama with her husband and a couple of cats.